9K10

G B B Hunter

D0996707

φin gin
AzR

1052

MEMORY

MEMORY

Mary Warnock

faber and faber

LONDON · BOSTON

First published in 1987 by
Faber and Faber Limited
3 Queen Square London WC1N 3AU

Printed in Great Britain by
Mackays of Chatham Ltd Kent
All rights reserved

© Mary Warnock 1987

British Library Cataloguing in Publication Data

Warnock, Mary
Memory.
1. Memory
I. Title
128'.3   BF371

ISBN 0-571-14783-6

Contents

Preface

'The most trifling objects, retraced with the eye of Memory, assume the vividness, the delicacy and the importance of insects seen through a magnifying glass. There is no end of the brilliancy or the variety.' (Hazlitt: 'The Letter-Bell' from the *Monthly Magazine*, 1831)

More than ten years ago, writing about imagination, I found it necessary to begin with an apology for writing so short a book on so large a topic. Apologies and explanations may seem even more in place in the case of memory. For memory is not only a subject of intense personal interest to many people, but it is also a favourite with philosophers. The branch of philosophy known as Philosophy of Mind has never been more lively, nor more thoroughly explored, than it is today; and within this branch, the twin subjects of memory and personal identity, the theme of this book, are front-runners. Psychology and physiology also have a stake in the topic. Nevertheless, I believe that just as in the world of music there is a place for short concerts, so there is a place, among all the literature of a particular subject, for a short book, in which one aspect is singled out for consideration. I have attempted here to suggest an answer to a particular and limited question: why do we value memory so highly?

In one sense the answer is obvious. Amnesia is a terrible affliction and can be crippling. Even common forgetfulness can have disagreeable consequences. We need and use our memories in every part of our daily life. But there is another aspect of memory, the reflective or recollecting aspect, which has a different and more mysterious value for us, and it is with this that I am chiefly concerned in the following pages.

Unadventurously, I propose an answer to the question in terms of our own continuity through time. In order to understand the importance of this experienced continuity, it is, I argue, necessary to make a great effort to reject the dualism, the split between mind and body, that has bedevilled our thinking for so long. There is nothing original in demanding that such an effort be made. Many philosophers, including among others Spinoza and Gilbert Ryle, have provided structures within which we might learn to think of mind and body in a new way, not as two quaintly related or uneasily married objects, but as one. But dualism is extremely difficult to eradicate. It is built into our language, and even the great advances in experimental psychology and neurophysiology which have marked this century have not, so far, succeeded in making us very much less Cartesian than we always were.

Memory itself cannot be understood as long as we persist in thinking of the mental ghost in the physical machine, neither can the peculiar delight and insight that we can derive from recollection. I have tried to demonstrate the nature of this delight and this insight by considering some well-known aspects of the poetry of Words-worth, and by a brief consideration of the theory of memory that was the inspiration of Proust's great novel. I have also taken examples from a variety of lesser writers who have quite deliberately given a certain permanence to their capacity to recall, in diaries or in autobiographies. An autobiography is the story of a life, and such a story can be regarded in two ways. On the one hand, it is the record of the comings and goings of a continuously existing animal, a live creature, who, being human, can assert and grasp his own identity from childhood until the time when he writes. But, on the other hand, a story has a theme, a plot and a hero. It is told to the world at large and can be understood by them. A good story has been worked on so that it conveys a truth. It speaks this truth to the world in general, not just to its author. And so the memory of an individual, encapsulated in autobiography, or in an autobiographical novel, has a general and universal meaning.

It is here that the functions of memory and the imagination are seen to overlap, or perhaps to become indistinguishable. The imagination, especially as it is exercised in the creative arts, is that which can draw out general implications from individual instances, can see, and cause others to see, the universal in the particular. The value we attach to recollection is understandable at precisely the point where memory and imagination intersect. Physical and bio-logical continuity and self-identity, ensured and asserted by memory, can be converted into permanence and universality by the attempts we may make to turn memory into art.

This is the area in which I have sought to answer the question why we value memory as we do. There may, and I hope there will, be different answers; but this is a start. I am grateful to all the people whose ideas I have shamelessly borrowed. I have had help from some, of whose fields of expertise I am deeply ignorant; and I would especially like to record my thanks to Anthony Storr and Professor

Weiskrantz for their help. I am indebted too to the Electors to the Leslie Stephen Lecturership in the University of Cambridge. The Leslie Stephen Lecture delivered in 1983 forms the basis of chapter 6 of the present book. Finally, I must record my deep gratitude to Jean Smith who made sense of my manuscript and typed it immaculately.

Mary Warnock
Girton College
Cambridge

1

Introduction:
Memory and the Brain

It would be generally agreed that memory is a mental phenomenon. Nevertheless, anyone writing about memory is bound to write about the brain, which is part of the body, as well as about the mind. And so to raise any questions about the nature of memory is immediately to raise in some form the problem of the relation between mind and body. It is worth asking why this should be so. It is perfectly possible to write about decision-making, or imagination, or the nature of humour, all of them in some sense mental phenomena, without discussing or even mentioning the brain. What is it about memory that inevitably brings in the physiological?

Part of the answer seems to lie hidden in the fact that we freely speak of other animals than humans remembering. We know that we can teach, or train, animals; and if we teach these animals successfully, they learn, and learning entails memory. Moreover, we know that quite lowly animals (or so we class them) like flatworms and octopuses can learn from experience. It is true that we sometimes also speak of animals deciding, thinking, or, in the case of favoured domestic animals, being sad or finding things funny. But we are aware of a danger of anthropomorphism when we speak so. There is a hint of metaphor. In the case of memory, on the other hand, there is no such hint. In saying that animals remember, we are saying something perfectly acceptable. We are not necessarily ascribing to them an inner life like our own.

The fact, then, that memory seems to be common to animals in general makes us less certain that it is a purely 'mental' phenomenon, to be discussed only in terms of inner experience. Though we may not believe, with Descartes, that animals are machines, working entirely as a result of influences from outside themselves, we do believe that their behaviour can be investigated scientifically from without. When we discuss other mental goings-on we tend to rely for evidence, at least partly, on introspection. In the case of memory we may feel less need to have recourse to such dubious methods. We seem to be talking about the observable public world; and this is generally taken to mean that we are talking about body rather than mind.

1

But even if we were to confine ourselves to the human memory alone, and refuse to allow that other animals remember in the sense that we do, it would still be very difficult to eliminate all consideration of the brain, as distinct from the mind, for we are all familiar with the oddities and paradoxes of memory. We can remember some things clearly, others, perhaps less long past, not at all. We know that concussion causes loss of memory; that old age, a physiological process, brings with it loss of memory of the recent past, but vivid recollection of the distant and apparently previously forgotten days of childhood. We have read stories of brain damage producing odd patchiness of memory, and of electric shock treatment resulting in amnesia. In our common acceptance, then, memory and the state of the body, and especially of the brain, are far more closely linked than is usual with 'mental' phenomena.

There is a further point: we are deeply and intuitively aware of the importance of memory to our own personal identity. But to think of memory in *this* way is immediately to think of it as both mental and physical, since it is so that we think of ourselves: composed of both body and mind.

So the language of 'mind' and 'consciousness' seems inadequate by itself to the concept of memory. This is greatly to be welcomed and is indeed part of the importance of the subject. It is high time that we stopped talking as if there were mental entities, or mental events, on the one hand, and physical entities or events on the other. The difficulty is, and always has been, to find a language which does not take such a dichotomy for granted. We need a language which does not assume that on each side of the divide there is something, and that the two different things are things of the same kind, like Oxford and Cambridge, or oranges and lemons. More than thirty years ago, Gilbert Ryle's great illustration of the Category Mistake, his attempt to explode the myth of the Ghost in the Machine and re-position the concept of mind was undertaken with just this end in view. A great part of Wittgenstein's *Philosophical Investigations* was devoted to the same cause. But, at least in the common consciousness and in the language of everyday, the old dualism persists. Because our ways of getting to know about the mental and the physical are different, we still find it hard to shake off the old questions about the relation between the two. Are mental events 'free', and independent of events in the brain? Do changes in the brain *cause* changes in mental experience?

Fortunately, this is not the place to enter in detail into the kinds of answers that philosophers, both professional and amateur, have given to these questions. I need only suggest my own position, in broad terms. It can be treated, for the purposes of what follows, as an unexamined presupposition, or prejudice, which will, however, have its effect on the total argument. I believe that mental events and events in the brain are in some sense identical events, not that one kind causes the other, nor that each happens coincidentally or in parallel with the other, but that they are the same happening. Such a view is widely held and is now generally known as Identity Theory.

I do not think that any statement of this view has yet been wholly satisfactory, partly because there is a quite general difficulty in expressing the thought involved. The thought is that what has been held to be two things is/are only one. Berkeley, and many other philosophers who have tried to argue that there is in reality only one world, not two, that there is a world made, as it were, out of only one stuff, have experienced this sort of difficulty. Moreover, any form of reduction is liable to seem unacceptably derogatory of that which is reduced: are you saying that all my profoundest thoughts and most treasured feelings are *nothing but* changes in the brain? Are you saying that real physical changes in the brain are *nothing but* changes in ideas? Nobody likes to be told that x is 'nothing but' y.

Another general difficulty in the statement of the identity position is that many mental phenomena (or 'states of mind') cannot be thought of as specific events. Memory itself, while not perhaps a state of mind like being resentful or being obsessed, is by no means necessarily a specific experience capable of being timed, or recognized as different from other experiences. Brain activity, on the other hand, lends itself to being described as a series of happenings or events. There is a problem about saying that a particular event in the neural activity of the brain cells, which could in principle be timed, is identical with something which does not seem to be an event or an occurrence at all or to have any time-tag attached to it. I fully appreciate this difficulty, which might be overcome if we knew more about 'states' of the brain, perhaps to be identified with 'states' of the mind. Even neurophysiologists seem to be very divided about how to describe either the brain or activity within the brain. I, at any rate, must be content with the assertion of a completely general proposition not confined to memory: it amounts to a statement of faith, that whenever there is a mental event, or a change, or an identifiable condition 'in the mind', that event, change or condition is *also* an event, change or condition in the brain.

A great deal has been made, in recent statements of Identity Theory (see, for example, Donald Davidson, 'Mental Events' in

Experience and Theory edited by L. Foster and J. W. Swanson, London, Duckworth, 1970), of the question whether or not the identity of some physical events with some mental events can or cannot be stated as a matter of natural law. I do not want to enter into this controversy, partly because I am not certain enough of what would count as connection by natural law rather than by some other link. But when I state my belief in the identity of mental with physical events, I mean this identity to be treated as a matter of fact, just as it is a matter of fact that the morning star is identical with the evening star, though there are two names involved.

As I have stated the Identity Theory in the baldest possible way, so I do not want to discuss all the objections that have been raised to it. There is only one which should perhaps be mentioned. It has sometimes been argued that mental states and brain processes cannot be identical, since brain processes are located in space and mental states are not. My thoughts about philosophy, or my sorrow at the loss of my pet, have no location. They cannot, therefore, be *the same as* a neurological or chemical change, which is literally *in* the brain, *inside* my skull. I mention this objection simply because it seems to illustrate the very difficulties already mentioned in stating the Identity Theory, difficulties which arise from the deep commitment, embodied in our language itself, to the distinction between the mental and the physical. Are we saying that there are two things A and B, the mental and the physical, which are in some sense the same thing (as it might be true, though it is not, that there are two universities, Oxford and Cambridge, but in some hidden sense they are really one, in that they have, let us say, only one charter)? If that is what we are saying, then I suppose it might be true that if one of these things is located in space and the other is not, it would be impossible to assert that they were really one.

But what the Identity Theory is asserting is not that there are two things which in some hidden way are one, but that there is *only one thing*, to be referred to either as A or as B.

Whether you refer to the thing in question as A or B will crucially depend, among other things, on how you get to know about it. You may get to know about it by, for instance, seeing it, or its effects, and you will give it, in this case, its physical description. Or you may experience it in some other way, directly, by feeling it in your bones, perhaps, and then you will give it a different, or mental description: you may talk of a sense of foreboding or a feeling of despair, something you know about 'from within'. But we generally have no possible means of applying any physical description to such felt 'mental' experiences. We cannot look at our brains, or even, as a rule, at the recordings of the encephalograph, while grieving for our lost pet; nor would we know what to look for if we could.

However, there is nothing intrinsically unacceptable in this predicament; and there are plenty of analogues for this kind of double description. If you show me some marks on a page, I see them, certainly, as physical marks, black perhaps, on a white ground, and of a specific shape and size. But I interpret them as an insult. There is only one thing in question, namely the set of black marks. I do not object that they cannot be an insult because an insult is not located in space and these marks are so located. I know quite well that the very same marks are *both* black and of a certain shape, *and* to be interpreted as insulting. Perhaps we should have this analogy in mind (though remembering that it is only an analogy) and try to think of mental events as interpretations or readings of events in the brain.

However this may be, the simplest and most bland statement of the Identity Theory, and one a century old, will express my general unproved presupposition. I quote from a paper entitled 'Mind and Motion' written by G. J. Romanes in 1885, and reprinted in Vesey's *Body and Mind* (*Body and Mind* (readings), ed. G. N. A. Vesey, London, George Allen and Unwin, 1964):

> We have only to suppose that the antithesis between mind and motion . . . is itself phenomenal or apparent, not absolute or real. We have only to suppose that the seeming duality is relative to our modes of apprehensions: and therefore that any change taking place in the mind, and any corresponding change taking place in the brain are really not two changes but one change.

Again, he says, by way of analogy:

> When a violin is played upon, we hear musical sound, and at the same time we see a vibration of the strings. Relatively to our consciousness, therefore, we have two sets of changes, they are one and the same: we know that the diversity in consciousness is created only by the difference in our modes of perceiving the same event.

And he concludes thus:

> If this most troublesome individual, the 'plain man' of Locke, should say it seems at least opposed to common sense to suppose that there is anything in a burning candle or a rolling billiard ball substantially the same as mind, the answer is that if he could look into my brain at this moment he would see nothing but motion of molecules or motion of masses: and apart from the accident of my

being able to tell him so, his common sense could never have divined that those motions in my brain are concerned in the genesis of my spoken thoughts.

I will take Romanes's words as a statement of an unexamined Identity Theory.

My interest in this twin phenomenon, memory, can best be put in the form of a question: Why do we value memory so highly? What is its role, not so much in our humdrum practical lives, where it is plain that we could not survive without it, as in the life of the imagination, in art and, above all, in our own self-esteem? I cannot answer the question 'why?'; but I hope to show the importance of memory to us by considering both what it is believed to be, and how it is used in our thoughts about ourselves and in the life of the imagination. To demonstrate its importance in this way might perhaps be to produce some material for a psychologist, a philosopher, or even a literary critic to use, in answering the question 'why?'

Let us start, then, by briefly considering the nature of memory, not as a specifically mental nor a specifically physical phenomenon, but as a feature of living things which can be classified as both mental and physical or, better, not classified at all. Only living creatures can be said to possess memory (and not all of these; but non-remembering, non-learning creatures need not here concern us). A living creature makes choices; and, however rudimentary these choices, they are made in the light of that creature's past history. To say this is to say that the creature learns from experience, or, in other words, possesses memory. Insofar as each living creature persists through time as a separate distinguishable individual thing, it can be said to have its own history, to live its own life. Therefore each has its own memory and makes its choices in the light of its own past. (We can include here its genetically inherited past, to account for the choices it may make by 'instinct'.) This is an obvious point, but one which will assume considerable significance as we turn our attention to specifically human memory and human life. We will think of memory, then, as *that by the possession of which an animal learns from experience*.

Now, it is very easy to fall into speaking, as people always have, of memory as a 'storehouse', in which things that may come in handy later are put away: a kind of attic or junk-room. So people frequently talk; but can we make this talk more precise?

In any animal, information is provided to it by the stimulus of outside events, but only if the nervous system of the animal reacts to the stimulus by treating it as a sign. Thus, if a rat learns to depress a lever, this is because he has depressed it accidentally at first, and a pleasurable sensation has followed. Thereafter the recognition of the lever is the recognition of something with significance. It is the *meaning* of the lever that has been 'stored'. A horse shies when a pheasant flies suddenly out of the field. Thereafter that same part of the field is recognized as a source of nameless horrors, and he shies again or is reluctant to go past, even though there is no pheasant the next time. The place is stored in the memory as significant of something bad. A great deal of work has been done on humans to clarify this aspect of memory, to try to discover the way in which certain items of experience become signs or symbols, the way in which they become information that can be retrieved and used. Much work has also been done to make precise the concept of location in the brain. Where in the brain is this information stored? How does transfer from one to the other take place? We need not concern ourselves with such technical questions, but attempt a more general understanding.

It used to be supposed that the physiological events of remembering or learning could be best explained in terms of chemical changes. It was thought that the records of memory were held in certain specific molecules which could, in principle at least, be transferred from one animal to another, so that if one flatworm ate its mate, it would now contain its mate's memory records in a literal sense (and this may perhaps be the view assumed by Romanes in the quotation above). There now appears to be little evidence for this theory (though experiments have recently been done involving the transfer of brain tissue from one animal to another, with marginally good results for the receiving animal, who seemed to become a bit brighter than before). Nowadays neurophysiologists seem to prefer the view that learning is a matter, not of forming new molecules, but of new connections between and within the nerve cells of the brain. Here again, exact evidence of changes going along with new or learned behaviour is sparse. On the other hand, physiologists now know a great deal about the vast number of cells in the cerebral cortex and the function of each cell to pass messages along the nerve fibres that stretch out from the central cell body, and also about the chemistry involved in this process. It is the subject that is perhaps most worked on, most fashionable, in universities today.

So soon we shall know more. For the time being, it seems reasonable to suppose that changes in behaviour resulting from learning (such as the rat's pressing the lever to get his treat) come about by changes in the connections between vastly numerous channels. J. Z. Young (*Programs of the Brain*, Oxford, Oxford University Press, 1978) says:

> human beings, like octopuses, have the power to continue to learn the symbolic significance of external signals even when they are adults. To our shame we do not yet know what changes in the nervous system enable them to do this; but we are beginning to recognize the characteristics of some of the complex stages that are necessary for the process.

These words were written nearly ten years ago. There is still, I believe, considerable ignorance of the details.

But whether there is ignorance or not, it is now fairly common to think of memory as a kind of retrieval system. The word 'memory' has indeed been used in computer science in a sense quite close to the one we want when we speak of the memory of animals. This use was noted in the second supplement of the *Oxford English Dictionary* in 1975. The computer scientist uses 'memory' to mean the physical system which allows for the setting up of a particular program. In a digital computer, for example, items of information are stored in particular locations, as answers to questions arranged by the program. The system works by the locations being found in order, very fast. The information from each location is then sent to a central processor, where the calculations are carried out. What information goes into any location is of course determined by the programmer. But there are also computers that, to a certain extent, provide their own programs, in that they can scan or search their environment for information of a certain kind, and locate each piece of information they find at a particular point.

J. Z. Young, among others, has used this model to explain the memory of living things. He writes:

> Memories are physical systems in brains, whose organizations and activities constitute records or representations of the outside world, not in the passive sense of pictures, but as action systems. The representations are accurate to the extent that they allow the organism to represent appropriate action to the world (op. cit., p. 12).

Here speaks the voice of pragmatism. The true and informative is the usable. Though there is much that remains mysterious in this way of talking it is probably becoming both more popular and more readily intelligible, as people in general cease to think of computers as themselves mysterious, and begin to treat them as part of the accepted and functional furniture of the world.

Nevertheless, such language, whether used of computers or, by analogy, of human brains, does not eliminate the metaphorical element in such words as 'store' or 'location'. Perhaps in time we shall cease to feel these as metaphors; or, alternatively, a better way of talking, more literal and exact, may be devised. In any case we should not be too completely devoted to the computer model, illuminating though it may be. For one thing, it may seem to be a better model than it is and so we may be seduced by it into forgetting our own ignorance. Secondly, and more fundamentally, there is a failure in the analogy. In computer science there is a clear distinction between hardware and software, even in the case of those computers which partially produce their own programs. In the case of the living brain this distinction cannot be drawn with any clarity. The structure of the brain cannot be thought of as something entirely distinct from its programs. Finally, whatever light the model may throw on the way the brain works in remembering, there is one enormous gap in the usefulness of the analogy. It does not explain the difference between memory which may work efficiently but of which we are not aware, and *conscious* memory where we know that what we are doing is remembering (see Daniel Dennett, 'Can we make a computer that feels pain?' in *Brain Storms: Philosophical Essays on Mind and Psychology*, Brighton, Harvester Press, 1981). It is as well, then, to bear in mind both the limitations of analogy in general, and, in particular, the limits of present knowledge in the science of physiology.

For it may well be objected that, in any case, all this talk about octopuses, rats and horses, to say nothing of computers, is irrelevant to our real concern. For in addition to the sense of 'memory' so far considered, namely that by which an animal learns, there is a quite different kind of memory, namely conscious memory, which consists of recalling or recollecting past experience. So far, all that has been discussed is the learning of skills, the ability to acquire habits, or, at best, automatically to recognize things as signals for action. But humans have another capacity, which is consciously to reflect on their lives and histories. This is the kind of memory that *must* be thought of as mental, not physical, for it must be experienced, and experienced privately, within the mind of each one of us. I cannot have your memories. Moreover, such memory must involve recognition that memory is being experienced. It is this sort of memory that is uniquely human, and is valued as such. *Memory-experiences* are what we should be interested in, and having learned a skill is not an experience.

I do not apologize, however, for starting with the sense of

'remember' in which we remember things we have learned, or in which we learn from experience and make our choices, like other animals, in the light of that experience. For one thing, however many kinds of memory there are, if one kind is a matter of certain neurophysiological happenings, then so are the others. Identity Theory must cover all kinds of 'mental' activities, not just some of them. But, more important, it is misleading to talk of just two kinds of memory, though both philosophers and scientists are prone to do this. There is a fairly general assumption that one can draw a line between the kind of learning-memory common to man and octopuses, and a kind of memory peculiar to man which is often referred to as 'event' memory, or memory of single events, which is different in kind. I shall refer to this distinction as it is drawn by philosophers in the next chapter. For the time being let me turn to a version of it drawn by Richard Gregory (*Mind in Science*, London, Weidenfeld and Nicolson, 1981). He writes as follows:

> Most recent experimental work on memory has been conducted with animals as subjects. This has the advantage that the individual life can be known in detail and controlled, but has the grave disadvantage that verbal reports are not available and so memories of individual events are impossible or at least extremely difficult to obtain. So experiments on animals reveal the learning of skills but not the recall of individual events though it is these that constitute our awareness, in memory of the past.

There is a confusion of terminology here which should be cleared up before we go any further. I entirely agree that we can distinguish broadly (though probably not in absolute terms) between 'habit memory', the learning of skills, and conscious memory, where we have a certain 'mental content' which we recognize as we have it, *as* a memory, *as* referring to the past (we shall return to this). But I do not believe that all the conscious memories we have are concerned with single events. Gregory argues (op. cit., p. 290) quite correctly that if we have learned a skill and remember how to do something like riding a bicycle we are not *conscious* of that acquired skill. We just do it. And we often cannot recall the learning of it. 'Although one has learned the skill of riding [a bicycle] we cannot recall individual events, the movements and so on, that led up to the skill. Yet the skill lasts for the rest of one's life.' He goes on to suggest that, while it is obviously their lack of language that makes it impossible for us to know whether animals other than humans recall individual events, it may also be the case that humans could not recall incidents from their own past, i.e. would have no memory of 'individual events', unless they had the use of language. This is to suggest that infants have no memory of 'individual events'.

There seems to me to be here both an unnecessary restriction and an unnecessary confusion. Learning from the past, whether by animals or men, entails a certain ability to pick out features of a situation and think of them as able to recur. This ability is the very same as that which enables a man or any other animal to treat certain features as significant. If features could not recur they could not be significant. Our nervous horse may see features as significantly recurring in circumstances not identical with the first circumstance in which he was frightened. If he has once been frightened by having to enter a horse-box, it does not need to be the same box in the same place that makes him react with fear a second time. If he had language he would say, 'It's *one of those* again. I shall have nothing to do with it.' This is like the case of a human who walks round someone else's garden and says, 'I see you have Captain Cook.' Not, of course, the identical rose bush that is in his own garden, but one of the *same kind*. Such identification of kinds is intimately linked with memory, both in horses and in men (or any other animals). If you look at an Osbert Lancaster drawing you may be delighted by the representation of 'Stockbroker's Tudor'. This is because you recognize the features of architecture you have seen dozens of times in your life but never perhaps so sharply. The wit of such drawings is dependent on your recognition of what they portray, and the giving of a name to what had never had a name before. You recognize the kind and then accept the word. The word is not necessary before you can recognize. Moreover you recognize in virtue of having seen this kind of architecture many times; perhaps you live in a house of that kind; or you drive past such houses every day on Western Avenue. There is no single event which you recall when you pleasurably recognize the architecture in the drawing. But you are perfectly aware that it is recognition; that memory, in fact, is of the essence of your pleasure. You have conscious memory, but not memory of an individual event. You have the conscious memory before you acquire the name. It is, I suppose, certainly true that without this kind of memory-in-recognition, without the ability to identify and re-identify things, there would be no language. But it seems wrong to make language the pre-condition of such remembering; and wrong in a different way to think of conscious remembering as always a remembering of events. After all, one of the most familiar, and, as we shall see, most highly valued kinds of memory, certainly 'conscious' and not a matter of habit only, is the way in which we remember places or people when we are absent from them. This may certainly occur without reference to any particular event. Yet it may be known and recognized, indeed deliberately cultivated, as memory.

This is the sense in which memory and imagination overlap and cannot be wholly distinguished. Both consist in thinking of things in their absence. If I am reading or listening to music with half my mind, as like as not I am thinking about, I am 'in', the close at Winchester. I remember every detail. Yet I am not thinking of any specific event. I have walked through the close a hundred times; I can recall certain specific incidents, a pageant in front of the cathedral, or a particular encounter with someone outside the south door. But I do not have to think of these events to be said consciously to remember. Half-living there in my mind is not remembering a skill like how to ride a bicycle. But neither is it verbal, nor tied to an event. Being *haunted* by a memory cannot fit necessarily into the dichotomy, 'learning of skills' or 'recollection of events'.

The whole question of kinds of memory may well be more complicated than has hitherto been allowed for. We sometimes remember individual events. We sometimes remember features of things and recognize them when they recur (and this may be done with or without the help of language, though when horses do it they have no language). We sometimes simply remember how to do things without any recollection of how we came to learn the skill. There are certain brain-damaged humans who have no experience of remembering a new event for more than a minute or so. Yet they can retain some sorts of information and learn from some sorts of experience, and react appropriately to what they have learned when it occurs again. What they fail to do is to *acknowledge that* they have learned it. They are like the equally damaged people who can in fact discriminate quite difficult things by sight, but who claim that they cannot see, but are just guessing when they make their discriminations.

It might be tempting to suggest that rats and octopuses remember only in the way that these brain-damaged humans do, that is that they learn from past experience, and react to the stimulus when it occurs again in an appropriate, learned, way, but have no awareness that they have experienced the stimulus before. They have no conscious memory. But recent research which has been much concerned with exactly this question does not give a certain answer. It seems extremely likely that, in humans and other animals alike, there is more than one system of memory in the brain.

L. Weiskrantz, Professor of Psychology at the University of Oxford, argues that recognition of objects is the first prerequisite for the survival of an animal, and that this is not a learned skill. Thereafter, and given this as a foundation, there must be at least two systems of brain function in normal human memory, and probably in other animals as well ('Categorization, Cleverness and Consciousness', *Transactions of the Royal Society*, 1985). Knowledge that something is a memory can be dissociated from skill-memory.

> For all of us it would seem that automatic memories are devoid of any awareness of being memories as such: we do not attach such a quality to our everyday words although these obviously have been learned. The neurological cases [the brain-damaged patients mentioned above] are useful and striking in showing how complete can be the integrity of skills of perception and learning in the face of a dissociation between them and the patient's own knowledge.

The next question is this: Granted that such dissociation is neurologically possible, how are we to tell whether or not in animals other than humans both systems are normally in use? It is possible that experiment and the observation of animal behaviour may be able to provide an answer.

But there is no doubt that, at the moment, we must confess ignorance of the point in the systems of memory where consciousness could be said to begin, and of how, in psychological terms, this consciousness is to be described. Professor Sir Andrew Huxley puts it thus:

> I do not at present see any way in which . . . consciousness can be related to the concepts of present day physics; physics does not contain even the right dimension for discussing what the relationship might be. It is clear that consciousness depends on the activity of nerve cells in our brains, and indeed that our sensations are closely parallel to the patterns of electrical activity in particular groups of nerve cells, but this is about as far as one can go. (Romanes Lecture, delivered in the University of Oxford, 1983, unpublished)

What is essential for an examination of the way in which memory is used and valued by humans is to grasp the complexity of the phenomenon. In some of our rememberings we may be simply habit-rememberers, like the octopus or the flatworm. In others we may quite deliberately recall things, not necessarily events, but places, sounds or the appearance of things, in order to give ourselves pleasure or pain. We may use not only our learned skills but our deliberate recollections to produce works of art or to communicate our thoughts in more humdrum ways to other people. It is over-simple to think of the memory as one 'faculty' which can be explained by one account. But it is not much better to think of it as two faculties. It is better to think in terms of a continuum, at one end of which is the mysterious phenomenon of consciousness. Some-where along the line animals must begin to know what they are doing in remembering. There is a distinction to be drawn at the edges of the continuum between habit memory and conscious memory. But neither is irrelevant to the other.

In what follows, since I am concerned with the *value* we ascribe to our recollecting abilities, it will naturally be with the conscious end of the continuum that I shall be concerned. For I am interested in the fact that often memory is not merely something which we deliber-ately evoke, but is also something that comes charged with emotion and is highly prized. But it is necessary to bear in mind the physiological roots of memory in the flatworm and the octopus. For we shall never understand the position memory holds in its grander manifestation in art and life unless we are thoroughly prepared to accept its connections in the systems of the brain. This is why it is necessary once again to make the attempt to cast off Cartesian dualism.

2

Philosophical Accounts of Memory

Philosophers have given different accounts of the nature of memory. Empiricists from the seventeenth century onwards have concerned themselves with memory as we actually experience it. For empirical philosophy, having as its aim to show that knowledge must, unless it is purely a matter of logic or mathematics, be wholly derived from experience, was obliged to examine the experience of remembering. What does the experience consist in? How do we derive knowledge from it? Can memory be trusted as a source of knowledge? These were the questions for the empiricists.

A good deal of what they wrote was descriptive. They were obliged to separate memory from other mental powers, and the test of the plausibility of their account was ultimately introspective. So, naturally, they were chiefly concerned with the conscious memory, that is to say with recalling. To recall is to have a conscious experience, and it was towards the nature and character of this experience that philosophers directed their attention.

Both common sense and philosophy are inclined to describe the process of recall in terms of images. When people say, 'I can see him now' or 'I can still hear the noise it made', they mean that they now experience something, as they might say, in their mind's eye or ear. And they might explain what they meant by saying that it was not the original sight or sound they now experienced, but an image of it. Thus, Aristotle said that, when we remember, 'there is something in us like a picture or impression' ('Aristotle on Memory and Reminiscence' in P. McKeon (ed.), *The Basic Works of Aristotle*, New York, Random House, 1941, p. 609). Centuries later, James Mill stated that when there is recollection of a sensation experienced in the past, the idea of it is not itself a sensation, but 'it is more like a sensation than anything else can be; so like that I call it a copy, an image of the sensation'. (*Analysis of the Phenomena of the Human Mind*, 1829)

This statement of James Mill's may irritate rather than enlighten, for it begs all the questions. We want to ask in exactly what sense remembering is 'like' the original experience. Not everything that is *like* something else is a copy or image of that thing. We have to decide, too, how literally our so-called images are to be understood as copies. We must ask what precisely is the relation between the experience we have now with that which we had then. Any philosopher who deploys the concept of the image in his account of memory is bound to try to explain how we can tell (if we can) that an image we have now is related to the past. How do we know that it is not a free-floating image related to no specific earlier experience? How do we know that an image does not relate to the future, rather than the past? Philosophers have realized that if they do not elucidate this relation, they will be left with a theory of memory that fails to make the crucial distinction, with which we are all familiar in real life, between memory and the imagination (close though these may often be to each other).

Associated with the imagist view of memory, there is a strong and natural tendency, referred to in the last chapter, to think of memory as a kind of storehouse. There is a spatial metaphor involved here, which we find it difficult to repress. Images, after all, sound like things, and if they are things, they must be somewhere, especially if they are to be produced when needed. How otherwise could they come to mind, either asked or unasked? Memory images are like guests. Some are invited, even sought after, others invite themselves, they are welcome or unwelcome. But guests have to have somewhere else to live before they come to visit. We sometimes speak of people as having 'well-stocked memories' as if the memory were a cellar. Other people have memories 'like a sieve', a notoriously leaky and unsatisfactory storage vessel.

Locke (*Essay Concerning Human Understanding*, Book II, Chapter X), as so often, boldly tried to adapt philosophy to common sense in this matter. He wrote of the 'power to revive again in our minds those ideas which after imprinting have disappeared or have been, as it were, laid out of sight'. He goes on: 'The narrow mind of man not being capable of having many ideas under view or consideration at once, it was necessary to have a repository to lay up those ideas which at another time it might have use of.' Just so one lays up pots of marmalade in the larder for future use, because one cannot eat them all at once.

Nevertheless Locke was embarrassed by his own spatial metaphors. His reply to an early critic, John Norris, who wrote in 1690, soon after the publication of the *Essay*, was an attempt to protect himself against too literal an interpretation of his earlier words: 'This laying up of our ideas', he wrote, 'in the repository of memory signifies no more than this, that the mind has a power . . . to revive perceptions which it once had with the additional perception annexed to them, that it has had them before.' This is almost the same as the account given earlier by Hobbes (*Elements of Philosophy: The First Section concerning Body*, 1655, part IV, XXV, 8 and 9): 'He that perceives that he hath perceived, remembers.'

So, on Locke's amended view, ideas are nowhere until they are revived. But then they are somewhere, namely before the mind. There may be no storehouse, but there is something like a cinema screen on which ideas appear, labelled either 'new' or 'secondhand', either 'original' or 'copy'. Memory consists in experiencing certain ideas 'and this we do when we conceive heat or light, yellow or sweet, the object being removed'. Memory is thus explicitly identified with thinking about things in their absence.

But we cannot recall everything at will. Locke alludes to this fact in highly figurative language. 'Sometimes', he says, 'ideas in the mind quickly fade and vanish quite out of the understanding, leaving no more footsteps or remaining characters of themselves than shadows do flying over fields of corn; and the mind is as void of them as if they had never been there.' But he does not pursue the question whether it is the constitution of our bodies or, as he suggests, the 'temper of our brains' which makes the difference between a retentive and a non-retentive memory. Memory is a kind of perception: Hobbes (op. cit.) had called it 'secondary perception'; and just as some people perceive more, and more clearly than others, so some remember more.

Locke (op. cit.) observes that this secondary perception is not always a matter of passively receiving ideas. Often the mind actively engages itself to seek ideas of memory. He suggests that even birds deliberately recall ideas to their minds and use them as patterns against which to test their success in learning a particular song: 'It cannot with any appearance of reason be supposed (much less proved) that birds without sense and memory can approach their notes nearer and nearer by degrees to a tune played yesterday; which if they have no idea of it in their memory is now nowhere, nor can it be a pattern for them to imitate.' So birds, and presumably still more often humans, hold a memory-idea in their mind and can compare what they are now experiencing with that memory-idea. Only in this way, Locke would argue, could we recognize something and identify it as something seen before, or practise a performance so that it approached the performance we heard yesterday. So the memory-idea must be sufficiently like the present sense experience to be compared with it. Memory, in Locke's view, though obviously to be distinguished from sensation, and derived from it, is nevertheless *very similar*. It is at this stage that the notion of a copy tends to come in. We *must* think of memory in terms of the perception of a likeness between an image and something more full-bloodedly perceived in the past.

This is the way of thinking which common sense, without aid of philosophy, tends to adopt and, as we saw, it is the view expressed by James Mill. The essence of memory is twofold. There is the present image-content, and the relation of this to the past. It is a particular way of representing things in the mind, things that are absent because belonging to a vanished time. Hobbes as much as Locke took this view. Hobbes argued that, without memory, we should have no idea of time. Both memory and imagination deal with the absent, or unreal. But 'Fancy and memory differ only in this, that memory supposeth time past, as fancy does not' (op. cit.). The distinction between memory and imagination is thus shown to be central to this empiricist's account.

David Hume addressed himself more explicitly than either Hobbes or Locke to this distinction. He used the word 'impression' to mean the experiences we have in sense-perception, and reserved the word 'idea' for 'the faint images of these in thinking and reasoning'. His use of the word 'idea', though supposed by him to be clear, is in fact full of confusions. It has to cover both what, in ordinary language, we might loosely call ideas (thoughts, propositions, speculations) and also mental images of all kinds.

In the discussion of memory (*Treatise of Human Nature*, Book I, Part 1, Section 3) it is the second sense that is relevant. Thinking about things in their absence is, all of it, carried out by means of ideas, in Hume's terminology; but where there is an image of the absent object, that idea is *like* an impression. Indeed, in this case, the difference between them is simply one of degree: 'The difference consists in the degree of force and liveliness with which they strike upon the mind, and make their way into our thought and consciousness.'

> 'It is not impossible', he goes on, but in particular instances they may very nearly approach to each other. Thus in sleep, in a fever, in madness, or in any very violent emotions of the soul, our ideas may approach to our impressions, as, on the other hand, it sometimes happens that our impressions are so faint and low that we cannot distinguish them from our ideas.'

If this possibility of confusion exists, then it must be possible for us sometimes to believe ourselves to be hearing a sound when, in fact, we are remembering it; sometimes really to see something and think we are seeing it only in the mind's eye. If this kind of confusion does occur (and I suppose it may), it would be a more complicated kind of confusion than Hume's simple language allows for.*

Hume realized that he could not leave 'ideas' so wholly undifferentiated among themselves. He had to produce some sort of criterion by which to distinguish ideas of pure imagination from ideas of memory. Unfortunately, in order to make this distinction he had recourse to the very concepts, liveliness and vivacity, by which he had sought to distinguish impressions from ideas in the first place. ''Tis evident', he writes (op. cit.), 'at first sight that the ideas of memory are much more lively and strong than those of imagination, and that the former faculty paints its objects in more distinct colours than any which are employed by the latter. When we remember any past event, the idea of it flows in upon the mind in a forcible manner; whereas, in the imagination, the perception is faint and languid and cannot without difficulty be preserved by the mind steady and uniform.' But this is very strange. For if even the ideas of imagination, described here as so weak and faint, may sometimes be confused with the impressions of sense, as he earlier said, how much more easily could the confusion arise between sense and memory? It is a wonder we ever know whether we are seeing something or remembering it. Not everyone has agreed with Hume, in any case, about the superior vivacity of memory. Hobbes who, as we saw, thought that memory and fancy were the same in essence, except for the additional idea of time annexed to the images of memory, nevertheless thought that they differed in force, but the opposite way round. 'In memory the phantasms we consider are as if they were worn out with time; but in our fancy we consider them

---

* Cf. Virginia Woolf, 'A Sketch of the Past' in *Moments of Being*, ed. Jeanne Schulkind, London, Hogarth Press, 1985. Virginia Woolf seems to suggest such a possible comparison between the vividness of images and impressions when she writes of her recollections of childhood: 'The strength of these pictures – but sight was always then so much mixed with sound that picture is not the right word – the strength anyhow of these impressions makes me . . . digress. Those moments – in the nursery, on the road to the beach – can still be more real than the present moment. This I have just tested. For I got up and crossed the garden. Percy was digging the asparagus bed; Louie was shaking a mat in front of the bedroom door. But I was seeing them through the sight I saw here – the nursery and the road to the beach.'

as they are; which distinction is not of the things themselves, but of the consideration of the sentient. For there is in memory something that which happens when looking upon things at a great distance.' Only here the distance is temporal not spatial.

But Hume had another criterion by which memory might be distinguished from imagination. This was a difference in the amount of free-play we might have with our images. In recalling something we are not free. We are bound by the necessity of how things actually were at the time when we experienced them. In imagination, on the other hand, we are free to alter and transpose, join and unjoin, as we like. He holds that 'the chief function of memory is not to preserve the simple ideas but their order and position' (loc. cit.). It is noticeable that here Hume thinks of recalling as a kind of action-replay; it is essentially concerned with events which occurred in a certain order. The memory of an event is not very much different from the event itself except that it comes afterwards.

The conjunction of vivacity and a fixed and given order which together characterize our ideas of memory, as opposed to those of imagination, is sometimes referred to by Hume as 'belief'. Belief itself is something to do with vivacity. But, in the end, he cannot analyse it. He falls back on saying that we all know perfectly well what it is. We know the difference between fact and fiction, between memory and imagination, between the real and the unreal, and that is all there is to be said. Experiencing something, remembering the experience, and imagining it if we have never had it, are on a kind of continuum of credibility. This is what Hume seems to be saying. The notion of the past itself seems somehow to have got lost in this account.

The twentieth-century philosopher who most closely followed in the steps of Hobbes, Locke and Hume in his account of memory was Bertrand Russell.* In *Analysis of Mind* (London, Allen and Unwin, 1921, p. 175) he wrote, 'Memory demands an image.' Describing the case of a child who relates something that has happened to him he said: 'It is clear that insofar as the child is genuinely remembering, he

---

* David Pears has identified at least two different theories of memory, both contained in Russell's early works (*Questions in the Philosophy of Mind*, London, Duckworth, 1975). My present concern is not to give a complete account of Russell's views, but to quote one further example of an image theory of memory. This, at least at one time or another, he held.

has a picture of the past occurrence, and his words are chosen so as to describe the picture.' But, like Hume and others before him, he has to try to distinguish the images of imagination or fancy from those of memory proper. For the child might just as well choose his words to describe a picture that was wholly fictitious. What makes his image a *memory* image? To be a memory, Russell says, an image must be accompanied by two feelings. The first is a feeling of familiarity, the second a feeling of pastness. 'The first leads us to trust our memories, the second to assign places to them in the time order.'

Although at first sight these two 'feelings' may look more hopeful as a criterion for classifying an image as a memory image than Hume's vague talk about 'vivacity', yet we may worry, as Norman Malcolm has pointed out (*Knowledge and Certainty*, Hemel Hempstead, Prentice Hall, 1963), because they seem too well-tailored for solving the problem. The 'feeling of pastness' is specifically designed to ensure that the image it accompanies is allocated to the past, not to the future, or to no time at all. The 'feeling of familiarity' has to be added to ensure that, once placed in the past, the image is accepted as an image of something that really happened, and that really happened to the child himself. For otherwise it would not be his memory. The image must not belong to a fictitious past, nor to the past of someone else. Hence the need for two 'feelings', both pastness and familiarity.

But if we try to analyse these two feelings further, to see whether they would, as it were, stand up by themselves, great difficulties arise. To take the feeling of familiarity first: if someone claimed to have such a feeling, he would probably be understood. He might be thought to be referring to the experience of *déjà vu* with which most people are acquainted. Briefly, usually for a few seconds only, everything that happens feels familiar. There is a sense that it has all happened before, and that what happens next will itself be familiar, when it does happen. But, of course, this feeling, though it sometimes occurs, is mistaken. We experience it when we have *not* had the experiences before. It is its unexpectedness and misleadingness which cause us to call attention to it as a feeling. It is quite unlike the case in which I tell you about my childhood, or about what I did last week, or brood on these things to myself. Russell recognizes the difficulty. It is logically possible, he thinks, that the world could have sprung into existence a moment ago and that what we think of as memory of the past is, in fact, simply a present image-experience with the addition of the misleading feeling that it has all happened before. It is rather as if you dream about walking through a familiarly frightening house, and in the dream you know that every time you get to a certain point in the passage, something terrible happens. When you wake up, you realize that you have never been in any such house in real life. But, you say, 'it *was* familiar: in dreams I have been there before. I have this recurring dream.' But how do you know? Might it not be that you have dreamed about the house only once, but that in the dream you experience not only terror but familiarity? The feeling of familiarity might be a phoney or misleading feeling.

A more intractable problem, however, is that, even in the cases where it does not mislead, the feeling itself, such as it is, seems to depend for its recognition on a previous understanding of memory. If I meet someone who seems familiar, this is only to say that I think I remember him. Even in the *déjà vu* case there is really nothing I can say except that it is *as if I remember* what is happening. One ought not to try both to explain familiarity in terms of memory, and memory in terms of familiarity. The concept of familiarity seems to add nothing to that of memory itself.

The same sort of difficulty arises if we try to isolate a 'feeling of pastness'. Consider the following case. A photograph, we may agree, is a type of image. Suppose I look at a photograph of a child on a pony, and I think 'this is how it was *then*', I have put the child and the pony into the past. But if I did not know independently that they belonged there, that one of my children, say, now grown-up, once rode a pony of this kind, why should I attach pastness to the picture? It might, of course, contain certain features which I know independently *must* belong to the past, such as a tram or a steam engine. But this is knowledge, not sentiment. As far as the picture itself goes (granted that it has no such 'dating' features), the child might be riding the pony still. The picture might be an instant Polaroid picture. My knowledge that the picture belongs to the past is knowledge based on memory. Whatever *feelings of pastness* may attach to the photograph, memory has to be invoked to explain such feelings. And what is true of the photograph is equally true of any mental image that may come into my head.

I do not deny that there may be feelings we have, which could be described as feelings of pastness or of familiarity. Indeed these feelings may occur in connection with our memories and may be important to us, as we shall see later, carrying with them all sorts of other feelings of nostalgia, of longing, yearning or regret. All I deny is that such feelings can be taken to be the *criteria by which to distinguish images of memory from other images*, and this is how Russell, according to this theory of memory, attempts to take them.

It seems that when we speak of familiarity we are already cryptically referring to pastness. I am familiar with the content of my image because things were as the image portrays, but in the *past*. For when we speak of pastness, we are referring to something which *did* occur, or which *did* exist in the real world. The characteristics of our images themselves cannot offer us an escape from the limitation of those images into the world they are supposed to represent, the real world we claim to remember by means of them. We seem to be asking too much of an image. Not only do we experience it, like a kind of faint perception, but it is being asked to identify itself as an image of a particular kind with a particular reference to the real world. It is as if every picture had to declare to us, as we look at it, what it is a picture *of*. Of course, some pictures do so, but others do not. We need extra knowledge, not derived from the picture itself, to be able to say, 'That is a picture of Aunt Fanny on her birthday'. This is a problem that faced Hume, not uniquely in the case of memory, but crucially in that case. He wanted to speak of all mental impressions as 'original existences', as experiences, that is, which just occurred, like sudden feelings of pain, or a sudden itch, without links joining them to anything else. They were supposed simply to form part of a series of experiences, following one after another. Yet, in the case of the impressions of memory, he had to show that they were linked to a real past, that they referred beyond themselves to this past. Anyone who thinks of memory primarily in terms of images will find the same difficulties.

There are, then, very serious problems inherent in the attempt to distinguish the images of memory from those of imagination by referring to any special characteristics possessed by those images. Nevertheless, we need not abandon the notion of the image as a part of the experience of recollection, even if its role is not so central as those philosophers so far considered would have us believe. If we reflect on the experience of recalling, it is obvious that sometimes we, deliberately or spontaneously, conjure up visual or auditory or tactual or olfactory images. It would be foolish to deny the importance of these images, even if we cannot use them to *define* memory, or distinguish it from other experiences. There is no doubt that they occur. Sometimes they may haunt us against our will. Sometimes, when asked a question, for example, 'Was he wearing a tie at breakfast this morning?' we may quite deliberately form an image, and answer the question by reference to it. If I ask whether you have fed the cat, it may be a vividly remembered smell, in the absence of any real smell, which makes you so sure that you opened the tin of cat food. There is such a thing, and we all know that there is, as recalling, in image form, what happened in the past, what we *then* saw or smelled.

But because of the difficulties we have encountered in explaining precisely how we recognize the reference to the past contained in such images, and also because we often seem able to recall things without their aid, there have been philosophers who have denied that images have anything specifically to do with remembering at all.

Thomas Reid, whose *Essay on the Intellectual Powers of Man* was first published in 1785, was a hard-headed, hard-line anti-imagist. Not only did he deny that memory was to be defined in terms of images, but he was inclined to deny the existence of the image altogether. Though we may think that Locke had tried to turn common sense into philosophy, Reid makes Locke look like a writer of science fiction. He, like Locke, starts from the presumptions of ordinary life, but he, unlike Locke, does not move far from this beginning. Thus, writing of memory, he says:

> Perhaps in infancy or in a disorder of the mind, things remembered may be confounded with those merely imagined; but in mature years and in a sound state of mind every man feels that he must believe what he distinctly remembers, though he can give no other reason of his belief than that he remembers the thing distinctly . . . This belief which we have from distinct memory we account real knowledge, no less certain than if it was grounded on demonstration; no man in his wits calls it in question.

Because Reid is certain that memory is a kind of knowledge, he believes that it is necessary to cut out all reference to images with which we have acquaintance as intermediaries between present and past. For if in remembering we were acquainted with nothing but images, we would never be able to get beyond them to that which they imaged. We would never be able to claim certainty that these images were the true likenesses or representations of anything else. And so no memory could be certainly veridical. Reid thus attacks the theory of memory as image, or idea, from the foundations. 'According to the theory', he wrote, 'the immediate object of memory is an idea in the mind. And from the present existence of this idea, I am left to infer by reasoning that six months or six years ago, there did exist an object similar to this idea. But what is there in the idea that can lead me to this conclusion? Or what evidence have I that it had an archetype, and that it is not the first of its kind?' Even if, he argues, it is conceded that an idea must have a cause, there is nothing to make us assume that the idea, the effect, is a copy or likeness of its cause. 'For then it will follow that the picture is an image of its painter, or a coach of a coachmaker.' The painter being in a sense the cause of the painting, but by no means like it.

Reid argues, then, that if remembering consisted in having a certain image we could not know that a particular image was a memory, nor could we know that, purporting to be a memory, it represented the way things were. But this is not the condition we find ourselves in. We all know what memory is, and we all rely on its truth. 'When I believe', Reid writes, 'that I washed my hands and face this morning, there appears no necessity in the truth of this proposition. It might be or it might not be. A man may distinctly conceive it without believing it at all. How then do I come to believe it? I remember it distinctly. That is all I can say.' He goes on, 'We are so constituted as to have an intuitive knowledge of many things past but we have no intuitive knowledge of the future. We might perhaps have been so constituted as to have an intuitive knowledge of the future but not of the past; nor would that constitution have been more unaccountable than the present, though it might be much more inconvenient.' We simply have to thank our maker, then, for the gift of memory, and it is futile to try to analyse the gift further.

Thus, for Reid, memory is simply a very sure kind of knowledge. He does not in any way try to connect it with our bodies, with traces in the brain, nor with our previous experiences. For otherwise he would not have said that knowledge of the future might just as well have been granted us. It is perhaps worth bearing in mind the extreme oddity, if not downright unintelligibility, of this position.

But without having recourse to the mysterious gifts of our creator, certain other philosophers wish, like Reid, to give an account of memory as a kind of knowledge which need have no connection whatever with images. One of the most influential, and certainly the punchiest enemy of the image, was Gilbert Ryle. In the chapter in *The Concept of Mind* (London, Hutchinson, 1949, Chapter 8, Section 7) devoted to imagination, he comes near to denying altogether the intelligibility of the idea of the mental image. For to speak of an image carries a suspect assimilation of thinking about something, with carrying a photograph or copy of it *in* the mind. 'The familiar truth', he writes, 'that people are constantly seeing things in their minds' eyes, or hearing things in their heads, is no proof that there exist things which they see and hear . . . Much as stage murders do not have victims and are not murders, so seeing things in one's mind's eye does not involve either the existence of things seen or the occurrence of acts of seeing them.' Ryle argued that Hume's attempt to distinguish between ideas and impressions by saying that the latter tend to be more lively than the former was a case of one of two possible mistakes.

Suppose first that 'lively' means 'vivid'. A person may picture vividly but he cannot see vividly. One 'idea' may be more vivid than another 'idea', but impressions cannot be described as 'vivid' at all, just as one doll can be more lifelike than another doll, but a baby cannot be either lifelike or unlifelike. Alternatively, if Hume was using 'vivid' to mean 'intense' . . . or 'strong', then he was mistaken in another direction; since while sensations can be compared with other sensations as relatively intense . . . or strong, they cannot be so compared with images. When I fancy I am hearing a very loud noise, I am not really hearing either a loud or a faint noise; I am not having a mild auditory sensation. I am not having an auditory sensation at all, though I am fancying that I am having an intense one.

What is true of imagination is equally true of memory, according to Ryle. We cannot say that a memory image is something roughly like, but weaker than, the original experience. Whether we are thinking of memory as 'learning and not forgetting', or, in a more episodic sense, as recalling or bringing to mind, the image, if it exists at all, cannot be central to what we mean. We cannot learn what happened in the past by looking more closely at our images. Even if we 'have' images, they cannot function as a source of knowledge in the way that archaeological remains or old photographs may. For Ryle would agree with Sartre (*The Psychology of Imagination*, London, Methuen, 1972, p. 9).

There can be nothing in the image except what we put into it. It is because we already know (have learned and not forgotten) what happened that we are able to recall it.

Ryle's second main point follows from his first. To say that we remember is to claim that we know what happened. 'Recalling', he says,

is a conning of something already learned. It is going over something, not getting to know something. It is like recounting, not like researching. A person may recall a particular episode twenty times a day. No one would say that he twenty times discovered what happened. If the last nineteen reviewings were not discoveries, nor was the first.

Wittgenstein unsurprisingly is equally opposed to the supposed connection between memory and images, but is less definite in his pronouncements. 'When I say' (*Philosophical Investigations*, p. 231) '"he was here half an hour ago" (that is, remembering it) this is not a description of a present experience.' With or without any accompaniment of memory experience, my claim that he was here half an hour ago is simply a claim to *knowledge of the past*. But Wittgenstein leaves open the possibility that the knowledge we get in remembering is a special kind of knowledge, that it may have a special feeling or flavour about it, even though we may not be able to describe this flavour. For, in passing, he compares our memory-knowledge (knowledge that it is the past we are thinking of) with knowledge, derived from sensation itself, that we are moving our limbs, or that a sound is coming from one direction rather than another. This is the kind of knowledge sometimes characterized by philosophers as 'knowledge without observation'. It may not be *incorrigible*, but it seems to be absolutely direct and without grounds that can be explained. Wittgenstein says (op. cit., p. 185):

> I may be able to tell the direction from which a sound comes only because it affects one ear more strongly than another, but I don't feel this in my ears; yet it has its effect: I *know* the direction from which the sound comes; for instance I look in that direction. It is the same with the idea that it must be some feature of our pain that advises us of the whereabouts of the pain in the body, and some feature of our memory image that tells us the time to which it belongs.

There is no such special, separately identifiable feature. Rather, in feeling the pain, we feel its location; and so, in the case of memory, in having the thought or image, we refer it to the past. Our thought itself advises us. Even though we cannot find words to describe this 'pastness', we could get someone to experience it by telling him to think about yesterday, or about what he has just said. Just so we might get someone to feel what it is like to move his hand by telling him to do it. Wittgenstein suggests that to think of the past, and to refer our thought to the past, are not two different things, but one thing. A memory refers to the past, necessarily; and we *interpret* it as containing that reference. That is what our thought means.

It seems, then, that the alternative to defining recollection in terms of images with a particular flavour is to define it as a kind of knowledge, knowledge, that is, with a particular meaning or sense of its own. Either way, by imagery or by intuition, memory is unique.

We are left, then, with the impression that there is something unexplained, indeed inexplicable, about the experience of recalling, which is a major part of what we mean by memory. It is either a mysterious past-impregnated kind of imagery, or a direct and unanalysable form of knowledge of something that no longer exists, the past. There are two more philosophers, both of them French, whom we should now consider. It would be wrong to say that they throw full light on the mystery. But they at least show us rather more of its nature, and lead us, perhaps rather more directly than the philosophers so far considered, towards an understanding of the central role of memory, both in literature and in life.

Henri Bergson placed memory in the very centre of his philosophical speculations because he used it as a prop for a metaphysical position, a dualism between mind (or brain) and spirit no less absolute than the Cartesian dualism between mind and body (*Matter and Memory*, London, Allen and Unwin, 1912, chapter 5). Just as Descartes thought that, though mind and body were two totally different kinds of substance, yet there must be found some channel of communication, some connecting link, between the two (and he hit on the thin and spirituous fluid of the pineal gland as the link), so Bergson regarded memory as the point of interaction between two totally incommensurable entities. Memory was to function as the bridge between the embodied, mechanical, determinate world of science and practical affairs, and the spiritual world, of which we are aware only by intuition, and whose truths can never be expressed in language that is wholly accurate or precise. Language, like our everyday consciousness itself, is essentially directed towards action. In order to act, to manipulate or change the world, we have to divide things up, label them, observe their interactions and relations, and encapsulate all these in precise description, such as will enable us to predict and explain. Our perception of the world, the perception which we try to express exactly in language, is, according to Bergson, a purely physiological phenomenon. But perception of the world, physiological though it is, is impregnated with memory.

His meaning may be illustrated by an example. If I perceive a horse, through the organs of sight, hearing and smell, I call on my memories of other past perceptions, which have, in the past, enabled me to learn what horses are like, and how I should treat them for my own purposes. The function of man, considered as a physical body, is practical; his aim is to survive. The particular function of the brain is, first, to receive and retain experiences, and then to release into present perceptual experience such memories as, when mixed with the purely sensory stimuli received, will be useful. The brains of all animals have this same function. In this sense memory is a neurophysiological phenomenon that has a crucial role in the survival of the animal. It is part of nature. Bergson held that all experiences are retained by memory, but only some are used. The function of the brain is to suppress or inhibit those memories that are, as it were, irrelevant, and let through into consciousness only those that are practically valuable.

Below the level of consciousness, however, there is memory of a different kind constantly at work. This is *pure* memory, of which we may sometimes, quite spontaneously, become aware when our brain's defences are down, as, for example, in dreams. In pure memory we are aware of something new. We are aware of what Bergson calls 'pure duration'.

In ordinary life, time is conceived always as a series, one thing after another, each thing separate from its predecessor and from its successor. Bergson held that such a concept of time is, in fact, essentially a *spatial* concept. We think of time as a set of items, laid out end to end. Such a spatial concept is indeed essential to our practical life. For, in practice, we have to distinguish one object from another, a tree from a house, a rabbit from a beetle, if we are going to be able to act, and to report on our actions, to say what we are doing or have done. The total grammar of our language incorporates and encourages this separation of one thing from another. Insofar as we think in words, our whole thought process is committed to a serial, spatial view. So we think of time as divisible into separate parts. One bit finishes and the next begins. The tree *now* standing, is *next* chopped down for firewood.

Pure duration, on the other hand, is fluid. It has no separable parts. Bergson speaks of 'interpenetration', like the beginning, middle and end of a melody. But even the musical analogy is not wholly adequate, since, up to a point, one can distinguish one note in a melody from another. Nevertheless it is true that to alter a note would alter not just a bit of the melody but, in some sense, the melody as a whole.

As soon as we form *distinct* memory images these are infected by perception. The divisive, space-dominated nature of our bodies, and the space-dominated concept of time, takes over and controls us. Within pure duration, on the other hand, we are free: our spirit, the medium of this kind of memory, is indeterminate, released from the causal necessities of both space and time. Somewhat confusingly, Bergson tends to distinguish pure or spontaneous memory from ordinary memory by using the words 'representational' and 'habit' for each of the pair. This pair of words might suggest that he is distinguishing recalling, on the one hand, from learning by experience on the other. And it is true that he starts with this distinction (op. cit., chapter 2). Remembering a Horace Ode, in the sense of being able to recite it, is habit memory; recalling the hot summer day when I lay on the playing field committing it to memory is representational. But later in *Matter and Memory* he places many of the representations of the past that we consciously and deliberately recall because we need them along with 'habit', and it is the spontaneity, not the image-content, that is made to distinguish 'pure' memory from 'practical'.

The concept of spontaneity itself undergoes certain fluctuations in Bergson's scheme. Often it is used simply to mean 'unconscious'. For when he speaks of our forming general ideas, for example, the idea of 'horse' by reference to which we identify the animal before us as a horse, he suggests that while we may consciously acquire a general idea from perceived similarities between perceptual experiences, this acquisition is itself based on similarities between experiences already stored in memory, though we are not now conscious of them. These similarities, he says, are not perceived exactly, but 'felt and lived'. Below the level of consciousness we are all the time becoming aware of likenesses and differences between our remembered experiences. It is against this background that we make conscious classifications, with the conscious mind.

In fact it appears that, in spite of having started with a dichotomy between 'habit' memory and 'representational' memory, Bergson ends with a concept of a continuum of memory stretching from the wholly pure, spontaneous and unconscious at one end, to the kind of memory consciously mixed with perceptions and actions at the other. The true dichotomy is between matter and spirit, with memory, in its various degrees, the link between the two. Habit memory is essential to our survival as physical objects in the world. It is essential both to ordinary perception and recognition, and therefore to anticipation and the manipulation of things to our own advantage. Pure spontaneous memory, on the other hand, gives us actual acquaintance with the spiritual, the eternal and the free. There are no mechancial laws in the world of spirit. Thus the distinction Bergson makes between the two ends of the continuum of memory does not correspond to the distinction between habit memory and recalling familiar to the Empirical tradition in philosophy. For spontaneous memory in its purest form can occur only when the brain's defences are down, when consciousness is inactive. Recalling in this sense might, in principle, be total recall, for everything is retained. It would be a pure intuition of how things are, and were, without the restriction of space, or of time which is assimilated to space. And hence the recall would have to be without language.

In the intuition of pure memory, we know ourselves. We are acquainted with spirit. But, unfortunately, exactly what we know can never be adequately expressed. For words themselves are physical objects, seen or heard, and they refer to classifications, based, it is true, on pure memory, but tainted with the perceived likenesses and differences of the physical world. Words immediately bring our duration into the context of the practically orientated physical world. The very syntax that joins them depends on the practical concept of time. Of its nature, the knowledge which pure memory gives, though instantly recognizable as knowledge, is useless and incapable of being shared.

Despite all the confusions, the shifting dichotomies and the rhetoric, there is much that is attractive, even much that seems true, in Bergson's theory. It has been claimed that he has had immense influence: whether that is so or not, undoubtedly he attempted to account for something which others have also wanted to account for. His assertion that, in some sense, everything is remembered, and that forgetfulness is nothing but an inhibition of memory, is a view which seems to be confirmed by physiology, even by psychology. But, more than this, his concept of spontaneous memory, if it does not explain, at least takes note of, the *feeling* we have about recollection, that it is significant for us and reveals our true nature. What is given in recollection seems more than trivially true.

Jean-Paul Sartre, not himself a philosopher noted for clarity or exactness, criticizes Bergson for the vagueness of his theory of memory. Perhaps he has in mind the ambiguity and slipperiness of the distinction between the two kinds of memory noticed above. But, as we shall see, he himself came very near to positing two kinds of memory, though, if anything, with even less clarity than Bergson.

There are two places where Sartre addresses himself to the question of memory, the first in *The Psychology of Imagination* (1940; English translation, London, Methuen, 1972), the second in *Being and Nothingness* (translated by Hazel Barnes, London, Methuen, 1969). I shall at this stage confine myself to the first account, though it is given only in passing. Sartre is primarily concerned here with imagination, but, in the course of the discussion, he distinguishes the images of imagination from those of memory, and, by implication, further distinguishes what might be called 'habit' from 'contemplative' awareness of the past.

The Psychology of Imagination was intended to be an exercise in the phenomenological method. Husserl, who attempted to use this method in its purest form, believed that if a philosopher could shut out all pre-suppositions from his mind ('put the world in brackets' as he said), and if he would then attend to the facts themselves as they are 'given' in inner experience, then he would discover, in experience itself, certain general truths. He would learn what constituted the essence of a phenomenon; common to everyone's experience of it.

It was the contention of phenomenology that philosophers such as Locke and Hume had been radically mistaken in their view of perception (and thus of knowledge) because they had not grasped what perception actually consisted in. They had started with the presumption that, in perception, I am acquainted with an idea or impression. They had held that, when I am aware of an object, whether in its presence or its absence, what I am, strictly speaking, aware of is this idea or impression. The existence of the object *of* which the idea is an idea, or the impression an impression, thus becomes problematic. For how do I know that *it*, as opposed to my idea of it, exists? Husserl held that, on the contrary, the existence of the object is not problematic at all, but is given in consciousness itself. For it is of the essence of consciousness to be object-directed. If my consciousness were not *of* an object, I should have no consciousness at all. Consciousness is 'intentional' of its very nature; and this is as true of imagination or memory as of perception.

When I think of something past then that past event is the object of my thought. There is no need to suppose that between me and the past event there is something else, my 'idea' or 'image' of it, standing between me and it. So far the phenomenological programme looks like a simple demolition job, a reassertion of common sense, such as that attempted by Thomas Reid.

Indeed Ryle and Wittgenstein, both demolishers of the image, were profoundly influenced by Husserl. But Sartre, being a more thoroughgoing phenomenologist than Ryle or Wittgenstein, was obliged to try to describe the actual experience of remembering as it happens, and to give some account of what it is like to think of things when they are absent, either in space or time.

In examining the experience of recalling, he found that he could not altogether exclude the existence of images. All he could do was to insist that images were very strange and ambiguous things, not at all like other things. In the first part of *The Psychology of Imagination* most of his examples are drawn, not from imagination, but from the images of memory.

He first considers the case where he looks at a particular chair in his room, and then shuts his eyes and recalls its appearance. From this simple type of memory image, he deduces certain general features of any image. There are four essential characteristics of the image. First, it is, as it were, transparent. I am not, in forming it, thinking of an *image* of the chair, but of the chair itself. But I am thinking of it in a particular way, distinct from the way I think of it when my eyes are open and I look at it. In speaking of envisaging we are speaking of 'a certain way in which consciousness presents an object to itself'. Just as we may, in thinking, present an object to ourselves by means of a word, and when we do this, we do not concentrate on the word, but on its referent (we think of its referent *through* the word), so our image is the means by which we think of the chair. It signifies the chair. Apart from its direction towards the chair, the image is nothing.

Secondly, the particular way of thinking in question involves what Sartre calls 'quasi-observation'. In thinking visually of the chair, in remembering what it looks like, we adopt the attitude of one looking, but we are not really looking. For the image can never teach us anything. There is nothing in it, Sartre says, that we did not put into it ourselves. In this sense the image suffers from an essential poverty.

Thirdly, when we think of the chair by the help of an image we know that this is what we are doing. That there is a difference between our image of the chair and the chair itself is an essential element of the nature of the image as we form it. 'However lively, appealing or strong an image is, it presents its object as not-being' (*The Psychology of Imagination*, p. 13). Simply having the image of the chair entails that we know we are not perceiving the chair itself. If our image is a visual image, as in this example, then an essential part of its being so is our knowledge that the envisaged chair cannot be touched or sat on. If we recollect the sound of an orchestra by means of an auditory image, then it is of the nature of the image that we know we cannot see the players. In memory, what we hear is something invisible.

Lastly, an image has what Sartre calls spontaneity. We know, in forming an image (and this he supposes to be true even if the image comes to us 'unasked'), that we are doing something. In perception we are passive. Things happen to us. We see or hear whatever presents itself to our eyes or ears. In imagining or remembering this is not so, we are in some way responsible for what the image is like.

So we do have images and we cannot give a complete description either of imagining or of remembering without reference to them. Is Sartre about to revert, then, to the standpoint of Hobbes, Locke, Hume and Russell, trying to distinguish imagination from memory by citing a special feature of the image in each case? Having listed the four essential characteristics of the image as such, the scene seems set for the introduction of something like the 'feeling of pastness', by which we may be able to distinguish the images of imagination proper from those of memory.

But Sartre does not take this path. He argues that images, though they may occur in memory, are not essential to memory. What distinguishes memory from imagination is not some particular feature of the image but the fact that memory is, while imagination is not, concerned with the *real*. Memory is one way in which we are conscious of reality. It is a kind of awareness of reality, whereas imagination is essentially a thought about the unreal.

> No doubt recollection is, in many respects, very close to the image, and at times we were able to draw our examples from memory to clarify the nature of the image. There is nevertheless an essential difference between the theme of recollection and that of the image . . . The handshake of Peter of last evening in leaving me did not turn into an unreality as it became a thing of the past: it simply *went into retirement*; it is always real but *past*. It exists *past*, which is one mode of real existence among others. And when I want to apprehend it anew, I pursue it *where it is*, I direct my consciousness towards that past object which is *yesterday*, and at the heart of that object, I recover the event I am looking for, the handshake of Peter . . . When I recall this or that memory I do not *call it forth* but I betake myself to where it is, I direct my consciousness to the past where it awaits me as a real event in retirement.

This is contrasted with the quite different conscious activity of creating an image of Peter as he might have been but never was, or as he might conceivably be in the future. 'There I grasp *nothing*, that is I posit *nothingness*. In this sense the imaginative consciousness of Peter in Berlin (what is he doing at this moment? I imagine he is walking in the Kurfürstendamm, etc.) is very much closer to that of the centaur (whose complete non-existence I proclaim) than the recollection of Peter as he was the day he left.' (op. cit., pp. 210ff). The passage just quoted is couched, it will be seen, in highly metaphorical and entirely spatial terms. We pursue the past 'where it is'. The past goes 'into retirement'. Nevertheless Sartre is making a genuine distinction.

On the one hand he wants to reinforce his general conclusion that the imagination is totally free. The ability to contemplate what is not, what in no way exists, liberates human beings from the bonds of the actual, and ensures them the power not only to think what they please, but to do what they please. They can choose to try to bring into existence that which they have conceived, but which has, as yet, no reality. On the other hand memory is, of its nature, concerned with the real existing world. Consciousness of reality is knowledge, and so memory is a kind of knowledge. Despite the fourth characteristic of images in general, specified at the beginning of the book (their spontaneity), it now seems that, insofar as memory consists of images, these are *not* wholly created by ourselves, or rather, we cannot create them in any way we like. Being concerned with the real, memory images *dictate* to us. We are, in a sense, bound by them, even passive before them, as we are passive in the perception of the world. Reality determines how we think of the past.

It is true that we can mistake an image of the past for a freely invented image of imagination, we can confuse nothingness with 'retired reality', but, in fact, they are different. That we may sometimes confuse, say, newts and tadpoles does not entail that there is really no difference between them. There is, Sartre would say, a negative element in all images: we realize that to have an image is to think of that which is *not* present to our senses here and now. But the nature of the negation is different in the two cases. The concept 'no longer' can be distinguished from the concept 'never' or 'not yet'.

There is perhaps a further distinction to be found in Sartre's theory, implied by him rather than fully expressed. Given that, in remembering, we are concerned with the past, there seem to be two different ways in which the past relates to the present. The implication of such a distinction is to be found in what Sartre says about anticipation, a mental activity which he treats as exactly parallel with memory. In a game of tennis he says (op. cit., p. 211):

> I see my opponent hit the ball, and as I run to the net, I foresee the course of the ball. But I do not form an image of where the ball will come. Its course is already contained in my opponent's movement. I interpret his movement in a particular way. The future thus gives meaning to what I see him do. Equally incorporated in his movement is that from which it arose, the shot of mine which he is returning.

Thus in all our experience there seems to be built both memory and anticipation, a knowledge of both past and future. But, Sartre says, there are two sorts of future. There is the living future and the imagined future. If I am meeting a train and waiting for my friend to arrive, I may not envisage his arrival, but that I am waiting at the station makes sense only because of the future event, embedded in the present. On the other hand, I may isolate the arrival of my friend, imagine how it will be, how he will greet me. This is the imagined, rather than the living, future of which I may conceive separately from my present acts. I could equally well envisage it if I were sitting at home. At this point the imagined future becomes very like the purely imaginary; indeed we are familiar with the way in which the one merges into the other.

If we apply this distinction to memory, it is clear that there is a kind of memory embedded in the present, essential to my understanding of the present and the future. I would not get to the station by 7.15 unless I remembered the way, remembered the time of the train and the agreement we had that my friend would be on it. But equally, as I stand at the station, I may separate for myself, or may find myself thinking about, what it was like when I was here last, of how my friend looked when he came off the train then, of what I was listening to on the car radio when I met him before. Here again the images of memory become very like those of imagination and the one may imperceptibly shade off into the other, moving from what it was like to what it might have been like. Nevertheless the difference between memory and imagination is that memory, like the anticipation of the real future, is determined by the nature of reality itself.

There is, then, in Sartre a distinction like that between habit memory and recollection. The first is incorporated in my practical and usable knowledge of the world. The second is also a kind of knowledge, for it is dictated by reality. I cannot simply make it up as I go along, and it is this restraint that enables me to claim it as knowledge. But it is a kind of knowledge that shares many features with imagination. It is this connection to which, later on, we must return.

3

Memory and Cause

The review of some of the philosophical theories of memory under-taken in the last chapter may incline us to the view that, though memory is often thought of in terms of images of the past, and though it is often, in fact, experienced through images, yet it may most properly be thought of as a kind of knowledge, to which images are not an essential, though they may be a frequent, accompani-ment. But if memory is indeed knowledge, it is knowledge of a very special kind; nor is it enough to say that it is special in being knowledge of the past. For we know about the past, even our own past, in many different ways; through being told about it, for instance, or through looking about us and seeing evidence of it. Memory, our own personal memory, is different from these other kinds of knowledge, and we must seek to identify the crucial difference.

The difference we are after may not be recognized, even in personal experience itself. And here lies part of the problem. Someone may have an apparently direct knowledge of the past, as clear, perhaps, as Reid's knowledge that he washed his hands in the morning, and he may believe that it is a memory when it is not. The reason why we say that it is not a memory is nothing to do with the quality or content of the thought of the past as he experiences it; it is simply that the thought is not derived in the right way from the past event he purports to remember. He may have been told that the event happened. He does not remember being told, but he does not remember the event either, though he remembers *that* it happened, and can envisage what it was like. My mother has, let us suppose, told me many times about the time when my sister hit me on the head with a book as I lay in my cot. It has become part of family mythology. I can envisage the scene as I hear it described, embel-lishing it with details of the appearance of the night-nursery and the cot (for these I do actually remember). I come to place the whole incident, wrongly, among my childhood memories. I was, of course, present when the event happened, but I do not really remember it. Again I may appropriate to myself certain incidents in the past about which I have heard, but which did not, in fact, happen to me at all, but to my sister. I recall them, in that I recall their being talked of. But, in fact, they are not, could not be, *my* memories at all.

The difference between this kind of knowledge of the past and true memory is not necessarily something that I can detect from within my own experience. It is a distinction that can be drawn 'objectively', from without. *You* may know, as I do not, that I cannot be recalling the incident I have appropriated among my memories, because I was not present when it happened; perhaps it happened before I was born. You may know, better than I, the derivation of my knowledge.

The philosophical accounts so far considered do not lay enough stress on the requirement for memory of appropriate derivation. The derivation of a memory must be, in some non-complicated sense, causal. I must know that the past was as I say it was *because* I experienced it thus, and not through the operation of any other cause. That such is the requirement seems plain from a consideration of the kind of cases just described. If I wonder whether I really remember being hit on the head with a book, or whether my knowledge of the incident comes from my being told about it afterwards, the question I am raising is precisely the question how my knowledge originated. Richard Wollheim discusses this point ('On Persons and their Lives' in *Explaining Emotions*, ed. Amelie O. Rorty, California, University of California Press, 1980), taking as his starting point a passage from Goethe's autobiography which is of prime interest to philosophers. Goethe prefaces an account of his earliest memory by raising the very question we are considering. Was it real memory or not? Was it a 'possession of his own' derived from what he himself had witnessed (and there is no doubt that he witnessed it) or was it derived from the report of another witness? Wollheim comments, 'What Goethe needed to know was how his current knowledge was caused.'

There are, however, several strong objections to speaking of the cause of our knowledge at all, whether this knowledge is memory-knowledge or not; and it is necessary to consider these objections one by one. All of them may be taken seriously, but none, I think, will turn out to be fatal.

In the first place it may be objected that we do not generally speak of knowledge as *caused* by anything. This is not a trivial or merely lexicographical point, but is intended to throw light on the nature of knowledge itself, and indeed does so. Investigations of the nature of experience must always start from a consideration of the language we use to talk about it. And so we are bound to consider the fact that if we ask for the cause of something, we characteristically do so with the question 'why?'. 'Why did the mayonnaise curdle?', 'Why did the engine stall?' We never ask this question with regard to knowledge. We ask 'how' not 'why' do you know. Knowledge is not the effect of a cause, and therefore neither Goethe nor anyone else can be thought to be seeking the cause of his knowledge of the past. Such is the first objection.

Since J. L. Austin's influential article 'Other Minds' (*Proceedings of the Aristotelian Society*, supplementary volume XX, 1946; *Philosophical Papers*, Oxford, Oxford University Press, 1961) the orthodoxy has been that knowledge is not a state of mind, as certainty, conviction, belief or faith are. If knowledge were a condition or state, we might properly ask for a cause of it. We might seek to discover what brought us into such a state. If I say that I am certain of something (or if I say I am in pain or feel afraid), I am referring to a 'state of mind', and you may properly ask why I am in this state, whether it is physical or psychological. But when, on the other hand, I say that I know something, this is not a report of an inner experience. To say that I know, is to lay claim to the truth of what I assert. It is to claim the right to be believed when I make my assertion. It is to profess to speak with authority. Of course people often make false claims to such authority. They say that they know things that are false, or for which, even if true, they can have no evidence. But this does not change the status of knowledge itself.

Knowledge is more like a piece of property of which we may claim ownership (rightly or wrongly) than it is like a sensation which we experience and attempt to describe. The question 'How do you know?' is thus not a question about method. It does not mean 'What means do you adopt in order to know?' It is not like 'How do you play the horn?' or 'How do you prevent the sauce curdling?' It means something more like 'How *come* that you know?' 'How is it that you are in a position to speak with authority?' 'How did you come by the facts?' This, briefly, is Austin's contention, and, though perhaps with some reservations, we may accept this account of knowledge as generally correct.

The objection we are first considering then is that, if knowledge is not a state of mind, it cannot be the sort of thing about which causal questions are raised. Therefore whatever Goethe was wondering, he could not have been wondering what *caused* his knowledge of the past. In order to answer this objection, we need to be able to show that the question 'How do you know?' despite its unusual form, is in fact a causal question. If, as I have suggested, it means something like

'How come that you know?', we need to show that this, being a request for a history, is a very important kind of causal question. But, before I elaborate this answer, I must deal with three other objections to the causal interpretation of Goethe's question.

Goethe's question implies that knowledge of the past must be causally related to that past, if it is to count as memory. A second objection to such a suggestion is raised by Ryle (*Concept of Mind*, chapter 8). Ryle is concerned, as we saw in the last chapter, to show that memory does not consist in the having of images. He argues, further, that even where images occur, we do not learn about the past by examining or inspecting our images. It is rather that we demonstrate or show to ourselves (re-present to ourselves) what happened in the past by the construction of an image to illustrate what we know. As part of this argument, in a somewhat complicated passage, he introduces the example of a person who reproduces for himself in imagery a naval engagement in which he has not taken part, but about which he has learned in some detail from those who were present at the engagement. This person is contrasted with one who re-presents the engagement to himself as part of his memory of it. He was there and took part; it is his genuine 'own possession'. The first man may always use the same images when he speaks of the battle, but he does so only as a matter of habit. The images stand arbitrarily for his concept of the battle, and he is aware that he could change the signifier at any time that he wanted to. The second man, by contrast, feels that he could not change his imagery of the battle. We are reminded of Hume who said that, in memory, our ideas are 'in a manner ty'd'. For, in recalling the naval battle, the man who was there is bound, according to Ryle, to recall it in a particular way. The repetition of his images, each time that he thinks of the engagement, seems to him compulsory, not merely a matter of habit. He cannot now, in recollection, 'see' it in his mind's eye just as he would like, any more than then, when he was taking part, he could actually see it just as he chose. It is this fact, Ryle argues, that makes it tempting to treat recalling by images as if it were itself a kind of looking or scanning. Both imaging the past which is recalled, and experiencing it in real life, seem to be determined by what is 'there'.

But, Ryle says, whereas the determination of the man who sees something is a genuinely causal determination, the determination of the imagery when a man recalls is not so. It is a logical not a causal determination. 'The "cannot" in "I cannot 'see' the episode save in one way" is tacitly assimilated to the mechanical (or causal) "cannot" in "the camera cannot lie" or in "the record cannot vary the tune".'

But, in fact, he argues, the 'cannot' is more akin to the 'cannot' in 'I cannot spell "Edinburgh" as I like.' 'Nothing forces my hand to spell it one way rather than another; but simple logic excludes the possibility of my producing what I know to be the required spelling and producing an arbitrary spelling in one and the same operation.'

The example is confusing, because it is at first presented as if there were a psychological or 'internal' difference between the two men, one of whom had, and the other of whom had not, been present at the battle. The first *feels free* to change his images, even if he does not do so, when he re-presents the battle to himself. The other does not *feel free*. He 'cannot' change them. But then we realize that, of course, he *can* change them. (He might be an imaginative or fanciful man, who wrote a short story based on the engagement, and constantly thought of it first in this way, and then in that.) But the penalty for changing his images will be that he is no longer recalling the battle if he does so. Psychology is nothing to do with it. If he presents to himself wrong images of the battle, he is not recalling; if right, then he is. But by insisting that there is no causal connection between the battle's having been as it was and his recalling it in a certain way, Ryle has made it impossible to answer Goethe's question. The man who was at the battle will get the images right and *we will say* he recalls. But suppose that he was at the battle, and gets the images right, but still wants to know whether or not he recalls? For Ryle *this* question, which was Goethe's question, makes no sense.

Ryle's next example, for different reasons, is no more helpful. We are told of a concert-goer who recalls that, at a particular performance, the violinist made a mistake, and he reproduces the mistake by whistling the misplayed passage. Ryle says, 'He whistles what he whistles because he has not forgotten what he heard the violinist do. But this is not a cause/effect "because". His whistling is not causally controlled or governed, either by the violinist's mis-performance, or by his own original hearing of it. Rather, to say that he has not forgotten what he heard *is* to say that he can do such things as faithfully reproduce the mistake by whistling it.' And so we are to believe that there are two senses of the word 'because'. One is causal; and if that sense is intended, we are to assume that the whistling is 'controlled or governed' by the misplayed passage. The other 'because' is logical. If this sense is intended and understood, then there is no reference to actual events in time but to a general necessary truth. What is being asserted is that 'remembering' means the same as 'being able to whistle what one heard, etc.'. Since the concert-goer is not forced to whistle anything, and yet since he whistles the error 'because' he so heard it, we have to accept, according to Ryle, that the 'because' we feel inclined to use in the explanation is of this general kind.

It would help, perhaps, if we left out the whistling of the passage, the overt expression of what the concert-goer 'hears' in his head (for he might not, for various reasons, be able overtly to reproduce the mistake, or might not wish to do so). Let us consider, instead, his hearing the mistake in his head. It seems far less obvious now that this is not caused by his hearing the passage misplayed at the concert. For one thing, he may feel strongly that it has been so caused. He may feel, to his annoyance, an inevitability about his so hearing it ('having it on the brain'); he may wish to shake it off, but fail to do so. He is 'in a manner ty'd', compelled to 'hear' what he would prefer not to. Moreover, when he explains his so hearing the passage, he feels himself to be making not an abstract general point about the meanings of words, but a particular temporal point about what happened to him yesterday and is happening today.

Ryle's dichotomy between 'logical' and 'causal' meanings of the word 'because' presupposes a simple kind of causation such that unless we can quite literally say that something is 'forced' (or 'pushed' or 'pulled') by something else, we must stop thinking of cause and start thinking instead of logic. So a true causal explanation must always, it seems, be a mechanical explanation. Clockwork is the great example of such explanations, and has been since the seventeenth century. The hands of a watch move *because* they are forced to do so by the cogwheels lying behind the face of the watch. If the watch is wound, the hands must move and will always do so, unless there is some visible mechanical fault or obstacle in the arrangement. It is because the concert-goer's memory seems unlike clockwork that Ryle, by his dichotomy, is obliged to accept the other alternative, namely that his explanation is logical. If this were the case, all the concert-goer is entitled to say is, 'If I didn't hear the misplayed bar like this, I would not be remembering.' But this is not what he wants to say. On the contrary: he wants to say that he hears the bar as he does only because he heard it so played. Nor, once again, is there any possibility of formulating Goethe's question in such terms as Ryle prefers.

Let us turn now to the third objection, which is, in fact, nothing but a generalization of the second, Rylean, objection. It is this: a causal explanation of any phenomenon, it is argued, is always general in form. It must always be of the form 'Whenever A then B'. Causation is a matter of laws, and laws must govern all cases of a kind. If we need to explain a single event in causal terms, we must bring this event within a classification and justify our particular explanation by reference to the general law that covers things so classified. Thus, if Goethe's recollection is to be shown to have been caused by his presence in the room at the time of the event recalled, we must be able to say 'whenever someone is present at an event at time t, then he will recall it, re-present it to himself or others, at time t^1'. Only if such a general law can be formulated, is it possible to argue from a particular representation at time t^1 to a witnessing at time t. But of course we all know that such regularity cannot be asserted. We frequently witness things we do not later recall, and we frequently represent things to ourselves and others which we did not witness; and even if we did witness them, we may, like Goethe, still raise the question whether or not we now truly *remember*. This objection is a widening of the Rylean objection, since, unlike Ryle's, it does not rely on a narrowly mechanical view of cause. It relies instead on *observed regularity*. But it is precisely such regularity, so the objection runs, that is missing in the case of memory. No law can be formulated to cover the relation between the past and my present recollection of it.

If we want to assert a causal link between the past and the recalling of that past, then we shall have to show either that no general law is necessary for a causal explanation or that, in principle at least, a general law could be formulated to cover the case.

The final objection to the introduction of the concept of cause into the account of memory (or at least the last I shall consider) is to be found in Norman Malcolm's book *Knowledge and Certainty* (Englewood Cliffs, 1963). In that part of the book which is concerned with memory, Malcolm maintains that there is no such thing as a special event, no timeable occurrence, which could be called a present memory-experience. (Here, as elsewhere, Malcolm follows Wittgenstein, sometimes into strange places.) There can thus be no question of a causal relation between present memory and the past, of which it is the memory. For to speak of cause is to speak of two events, one of which brings about the other. But memory is nothing but the retention of knowledge. There are not two events which could be related to each other, causally or in any other way. There is just one event, which took place in the past. So far, this objection looks very like the first objection, considered above (p. 38). But Malcolm adds a further point. For he argues that when the past event occurred I knew that it occurred, and now, in the present, I still know that it did. My present knowledge is the very same as the knowledge I had then.

This objection, and the theory that lies behind it, leads to some very odd consequences. They have been noticed and thoroughly discussed by C. B. Martin and Max Deutscher ('Remembering', *Philosophical Review*, 1966). On Malcolm's theory, I cannot be said to remember anything unless I knew that it was happening at the time when it happened. In order for this to be plausible, we have to interpret 'knowledge' in a very liberal way. On a liberal interpretation, I may be said to have known that something was happening as long as I was conscious that something was happening, even if I did not know at the time *what* was happening, or how to describe it. On such an interpretation of knowledge we can allow that I may remember something, now described by me as 'indigestion' or 'sexual curiosity' or 'the last sight I ever had of the *Queen Mary*' which, though I experienced it in the past and was conscious of the experience, I did not know how to describe.

But Malcolm himself will not permit such a liberal interpretation. For he wants the knowledge I have now in remembering to be 'the same' knowledge as I had then in experiencing, in a very precise sense. He insists that, unless I could then describe what was happening, I could not be said to have known that it was happening. And if I did not know then, I cannot have the same knowledge now as I had then; that is to say, I cannot remember. He says, 'I do not believe that there is any sense in which a dog or an infant can be said to know that it has some sensation. I accept the consequence that a dog cannot be said to remember that he had a painful ear, and also the more interesting consequence that a human being cannot be said to remember that he had one, if he had it at a time before he know enough language to tell anyone that he had it.' We are reminded of Richard Gregory's suggestion (see chapter 1, p. 10) that one cannot recall an incident unless one has the language in which to express the recall. Malcolm goes further. Not only does the concept of memory demand that there must now be language in which to describe the then incident, but there must *have been* language in which to describe it then, when it happened.

The consequence which Malcolm is prepared to accept as 'interesting' is one that must be rejected by common sense. Indeed it is the premise upon which the whole of the present investigation rests, that all animals (or at least all with a central nervous system) remember things, and that human recalling is only a special case of the general multi-systemed phenomenon of remembering. So if Malcolm's 'interesting' consequence necessarily follows from his theory that memory is knowledge, then we shall have to reject his theory as well, through its *reductio ad absurdum*. But, in fact, the consequence follows only from his version of the theory that memory is knowledge, namely the version that insists that memory is *the same* knowledge which the remembering subject had then and still has now. It is this aspect of the theory that we shall have to reject in the name of common sense.

Malcolm allows that to say of someone that he remembers may be to say that he knows now *because* he knew then. But, like Ryle, he insists that the 'because' in this expression does not refer to a causal connection. It has, he argues, a negative function. It means only that nothing has happened between 'then' and 'now' which really caused the present knowledge. The person in question has not, for example, just learned what he claims to remember, nor has he been reminded of it. If someone says, 'I know now because you reminded me' he is, according to Malcolm, uttering a genuinely causal statement. But if he cannot say this, and can say only, 'I know now because I knew then', there is no causal link, and the sense of the word 'because' has changed. In a causal account of anything, Malcolm claims, there must be a 'gap' between the cause and its alleged effect. At the least the two must be conceptually separable from each other. So if I inform you that the cause of the failure of my car to start is the sudden damp weather, it must be possible to think of these two things, the cause and the effect, separately from one another. They are two, as it were, free-standing phenomena. But, Malcolm argues, in the case of true recalling, there is no such conceptual gap. Indeed he holds that the concept of any such gap between the original event and my recollection of it is a piece of mystification, a part of the 'metaphysical aspect of the topic of memory'. We cannot, he says, imagine what might fill any gap between my past knowledge and my present knowledge. 'In a sense then we do not know what it means to speak of a gap here.'

In spite of the authoritative echoes of Wittgenstein in the above quotation (especially in the characteristic use of the word 'here'), what Malcolm says is great rubbish. We know perfectly well what we mean by the gap between my knowledge then and my knowledge now. It is the most obvious gap in the world: that between the past and the present. It is a temporal gap. The very words 'past' and 'present', implicit in our concept of recollection, point to the existence of this gap. When Goethe asked his question, he was asking whether he now knew about the past because he remembered it or because he had been told, and he was not asking which of two senses of the word 'because' he was employing. He was using one unequivocal sense of the word. He was asking, that is, whether the past was itself the cause or source of his present knowledge.

Malcolm considers the use of the word 'source' in this connection, and tries the same method as he used with 'because'. The 'source' of present knowledge, he says, must be understood in a purely negative sense. If there has been no other event that has given rise to my knowledge, distinct from the original knowledge I had of it when it occurred, then I can speak of my original knowledge as the 'source' of my present knowledge. But I must not suppose that 'source' has any causal implications in this case (though it would have causal implications if the source of my knowledge was that you had whispered it in my ear). For to suppose a causal implication would, once again, imply a gap between the past and the present; and it is this gap that he is at pains to deny.

So much for the objections. I want now to reinstate the possibility of a causal answer to Goethe's question. I must do this by considering a bit further the nature of causation itself, and its many varieties, though I can do this only sketchily. It will turn out not to be a pointless digression. For the nature of the causal connection between present recollection and past events will ultimately throw light, not only on the nature of memory as we experience it, but, more important, on the value that we ascribe to it.

In pursuit of this end, we must turn to an important article by Elizabeth Anscombe entitled 'Memory, "Experience" and Causation' (*Contemporary British Philosophy*, ed. H. D. Lewis, London, George Allen and Unwin, 1974). Elizabeth Anscombe argues that there is no specially identifiable experience of recalling. There is, that is to say, no event occupying a specific time to stand as the central defining feature of memory. But, she concludes, memory is not simply knowledge of the past. It is knowledge caused by the past; and she proceeds to discuss the nature of the causation involved.

> We should clear our minds of all prejudice on the subject of causality in considering what we know here. Here is someone . . . who knows that such-and-such occurred. Let us suppose that this is a surprising fact . . . we want an explanation. How *has it come about that* this person knows that? we ask and then we are convincingly told: 'Well he was there. He witnessed it.' The mystery is removed: we are no longer puzzled about what brought about this state of affairs which surprised us so much. This is an original phenomenon of causality: one of its types whether or not anyone has yet classified it as such. No general theory of what causality is has to be introduced to justify acceptance of it.

And later she writes:

> The original witnessing of a remembered event is a cause of any
> present memory of that event. And this may be seen as 'analytic' (a
> logical truth, as Ryle would have it). Not so if, instead of speaking of
> memory, we speak of present knowledge of or belief about a past
> event. An affirmative answer to the question whether the *source* of a
> man's present knowledge was his having witnessed the event is
> enough to determine that the knowledge is memory. This is part
> and parcel of how we use the word 'memory'. But also of how we
> use the word 'source' in connection with knowledge.

Thus the causal connection between memory and the past is not only
allowed but insisted on by Elizabeth Anscombe. It is a connection
contained in the word 'source'. We answer the question 'How do
you know?' by reference to sources of knowledge; and this question,
though unusual in form, turns out to be indeed a causal question,
requiring a causal answer. If we want to know whether or not a
man, Goethe or another, *remembers* on a particular occasion of his
claiming to know not only *that* something occurred in the past, but
how it was, what it was like, then we are asking a causal question
relating to this particular occasion, when he makes the claim.

Must we therefore say that this kind of question is unique,
referring to a unique kind of cause? This is what Elizabeth Anscombe
suggests. She refers to the causality involved as 'an original phenomenon of causality'. She demands that we put out of our minds all
prejudices about the general nature of causality. She may even hold
that there is nothing more to be said about this kind of cause. It just
occurs, and, in real life, we accept that it does. I would hope that
something more could be said, even without embarking on a
full-blown theory of causality.

Russell, as Elizabeth Anscombe notices, had, long before, tenta-
tively suggested a special type of causation, operative only in the case
of memory; or rather he had thought it worthwhile to invent a
special term, 'mnemonic cause', to cover the relation between past
event and present memory (*Analysis of Mind*, London, George Allen
and Unwin, 1921, pp. 85ff.). In the passage we are concerned with,
he was speaking of memory, not in the sense of recollection, but in a
general sense appropriate to all animals, including man. He wrote,
'Whenever the effect resulting from a stimulus to an organism differs
according to the past history of the organism without our being able
to detect any relevant difference in the present structure, we will
speak of "mnemonic causation".' Thus if an octopus withdraws from

a stimulus today, having experienced yesterday that it was painful, we can speak of its behaviour being 'mnemonically caused', there being nothing else different about today's stimulus and response except that it followed yesterday's. Similarly, if someone asks me about an event in the past, providing me with a 'reminding' stimulus, and if I answer spontaneously in a way that I would not have answered if I had not witnessed the event, we are also to speak of mnemonic causation. Russell regarded such language as provisional. He was strongly inclined to believe that, one day, a series of physiological facts would be discovered which would entitle us to speak of physiological causes in such cases. These causes would be, he thought, something like 'engrams' or 'traces'; and if we understood them they would provide an intelligible link between the past and the present, and would remove the necessity for a special sense of 'cause' to provide the link. But, he held, such explanations in terms of physiology were, at the time of writing, too hypothetical to be used. Thus to speak of 'mnemonic cause' as a special kind of cause was a species of shorthand. It referred, he held, to that element needed in any account of memory to connect the present with the past. It meant 'some causal link, we know not what'.

The trouble with such a coinage as 'mnemonic cause' is, as Russell well understood, that it inevitably disappoints. It promises more than it can deliver in the way of explanation. It is rather like saying that it is my jealous nature that causes me to think jealous thoughts; or that it is the tendency to fall downwards that causes the apple to descend from the tree. It is suspiciously easy to answer the question 'How is your present thought linked with the past?' with the all-too-well-fitted reply 'By mnemonic causality.' Russell could even have used the same magic formula to account for the otherwise mysterious 'feeling of familiarity' which as we saw (see chapter 2) he sometimes thought must attach to any memory image called up in recollection. We seem not to have advanced beyond the point of saying that, in memory, the present is linked with the past *somehow*.

Does Elizabeth Anscombe's so-called 'original phenomenon of cause', then, fare any better than Russell's mnemonic cause? It may seem that it does not. If we try to argue that two things are linked to each other as cause and effect, but that the causal link exemplified is peculiar to the case in question, or even to the type of case in question, this must, it seems, inevitably fall short as an explanation. For to explain is to place something less well understood in a relation to something better understood, either by showing that the former is a kind or species of the latter, or, at the very least, that there is a strong analogy between the two. Elizabeth Anscombe seems to refuse to allow any such relating of memory-cause to cause in general. She speaks of the relation between the past witnessing of an event and its subsequent recall as *unique*. And so her answer to the question 'How is the present memory related to the past?' seems, after all, to be no answer, especially as she denies that there is any event, a present memory-experience, to be the effect, in the ordinary sense, of a cause. Once again it looks as if we might as well be content with the statement that the past and the present are related *somehow*. We are not allowed to bring the relation into a wider category of causal relations in general.

However, in the course of her argument, Elizabeth Anscombe refers to the past event as 'the source' of the present memory. And this in itself is to bring the causal connection out of its isolation, and into line with causal connections that are perfectly familiar. In urging her readers to lay aside all presuppositions with regard to the nature of causality in general, she is urging them not to assume that causal connections must always be capable of being expounded in terms of regularity rules or causal laws (compare the third objection above, p. 42). Many of our most familiar causal explanations seem to be far from such law-like regularity; it seems that we do not have to think of laws before we can understand them, nor do we have to be able to formulate anything approaching such a law. We are perfectly accustomed to explaining my laughter in terms of the words I have just heard you utter (and 'What you said made me laugh' is a perfectly good causal explanation); or my catching cold in terms of the cold you had last week. In neither of these cases would we be able to formulate a law; yet the explanation in each case is both causal and intelligible. Why, then, does Elizabeth Anscombe find it necessary to warn us against prejudice, and then introduce a totally new, unique kind of causality, to account for the relation between past and present in memory?

Perhaps she is afraid that we all, like Ryle, think of cause as *really* mechanical, a matter of pushing and pulling, of exerting forces which, even if we could not formulate a covering law ourselves, we believe could be encapsulated in a law, of the form 'whenever A then B'. There is no doubt that such a model of cause has a strong influence on our thought, and it may well be from such 'mechanical' examples that we all of us draw our first notions of cause, and of causal explanation. We know, from an early age, that by moving we can make other things move, that we ourselves, moreover, can be pushed and pulled and picked up by superior forces. Elizabeth

Anscombe herself is prepared to endorse some such view. In an essay entitled 'Causality and Determination' (Inaugural Lecture to Cambridge University, Cambridge, 1971) she writes:

> The truthful answer to the question 'How did we come by our primary notion of causality?' is that in learning to speak we learned the linguistic representation and application of a host of causal concepts . . . the word 'cause' can be added to a language in which are already represented many causal concepts. A small selection: scrape, push . . . burn, knock over, squash, make, hurt. As surely as we learn to call people by name or to report from seeing it that the cat was on the table, we also learned from having observed it that someone drank up the milk or that the dog made a funny noise or that things were cut or broken, by whatever we saw cut and break them.

Although she regards such remarks as 'unhelpful' in a philosophical discussion of cause, they are nevertheless significant, and may account for our prejudice in favour of the mechanical, the observable and the regular in our causal explanations.

But when we move from the simplicities of cutting, pushing, pulling, or knocking over, causal explanations are inevitably metaphorical. Many of our metaphors of cause preserve the mechanical within themselves. Hence the enormous popularity, both with ordinary people and with high court judges, of the metaphor of the causal chain (see H.L.A. Hart and A.M. Honore, *Causation and the Law*, Oxford, 1959) which can be broken only by an *act of breaking the chain*, the *novus actus interveniens*. There are other metaphors too, and one of the most powerful and useful of these is the metaphor of the source. Rivers properly have sources, but so, in our explanatory talk, do infections; so do revolutions; so does discontent; so does anxiety. And so, as Elizabeth Anscombe acknowledges, does knowledge.

If I tell you that the source of my knowledge is that I was there, and saw what happened, I have given a causal explanation of my knowledge, and one of a perfectly familiar kind. I have simply embraced a causal metaphor that is different from the mechanical metaphor which Elizabeth Anscombe wishes us to avoid, and which Ryle, for one, seems to regard as the only possible picture of causation.

It may be objected that to speak in terms of causal *metaphors* is to avoid the issue. Why should we be committed to metaphor, in talking about causality? How are we supposed to know what is a good metaphor and what a bad one? If some causal metaphors work and others don't, is this not itself proof that there exists a *central core meaning* of the word 'cause'? If so, we ought to seek out this central, literal, meaning, and, having found it, ask whether past experience of an event did or did not cause present knowledge of it, whether in Goethe's case or another.

There are many problems involved in this objection; but the main, though imprecise, answer to it is this: in dividing the world into causes and effects we are not dividing it once and for all into different kinds of things, nor are we judging the world in a way that is ultimately susceptible of proof. The concept of cause is a practical concept, used because it is useful. One of the things we need to know about the world is what makes things happen (or, in a specific instance, what made this happen). Here the model of clockwork, of cogwheels or of chains, is wonderfully simple and visible. But another thing we need to know is 'Where did it start?' Or 'How did it come into existence?' And here the typical instance, the pattern, may well be the seed which, when planted, grew into the lettuce, or the source which, springing up from the ground, turned into the river. There may be other causal metaphors, but these are the commonest, the most useful, and so the most explanatory.

Considering these metaphors, there is one further feature of them to be noticed, a feature they have in common. In the case of the causal chain, the great central metaphor of mechanical causation, the beauty of the metaphor is the visible continuity between one end of the chain and the other. Each link is physically connected with the next, and if the links fall apart, if the chain is cut, the occurrences at one end of the chain have no further effect on the occurrences at the other end. Continuity is afforded by the chain, in this case a physical and spatial continuity. Even if we change the metaphor and talk about sources, continuity is still demanded. We will not think of the spring as the source of the river unless we believe that somewhere, even if invisible, perhaps underground, the water is continuous with the water we later identify as the river. The continuity in such a case is more complicated and more obscure . . . But that there is physical continuity is implicit in the use of the word 'source'. We perhaps prefer the visible or felt continuity of clockwork, or the links in the chain. But where clockwork looks implausible, the continuity of the water, continuously flowing from the source to the river mouth, is quite good instead. And so if a man's being present at a particular scene can be thought of as the *source* of his knowledge (in the case when he remembers and has not been told) then there is, written into this metaphor, the notion of continuity between then and now, a physical continuity between past and present.

So I believe that, even if we cannot yet explain the physiological happenings which bring it about that a man can *now* claim to know what he *then* witnessed (nor what differentiates this case from the case when he was there, witnessed what occurred, but retains no knowledge of it afterwards), the kind of causation referred to by saying that in the first case his witnessing was the source of his knowledge is not wholly different from the kind that would be employed if we knew more of the physiology. If we could give an accurate account of what happened in his eyes, his ears and his brain when he witnessed the event and then recalled it, we should obviously and overtly be asserting his continuity then and now. But even short of such an account, in saying that what he witnessed was the source of his knowledge, we are *presuming* just such continuity. We do not need to suppose a totally new and mysterious kind of causation to account for the causal connection between then and now. All we need is the *history of the man*; and that would, if we knew more, include the history of his eyes, his ears and his brain. Then, when we asked him for the source of his knowledge, we should, as we often are, be asking for the story of his life, but a rather more detailed story than we can have at present. That his life has a story is something we take for granted, just as we take for granted the continuity implied in the metaphor of the source.

This same continuity is also present by implication in the further metaphor of memory, that of the storehouse, wherein experiences are laid up for future use. We have seen already how seductive that metaphor has always been. It is now time to examine further the notion of *continuity*. For this, while central to the causal account of memory-knowledge, is also central to the idea of memory itself, and especially to the value we ascribe to it.

4

Personal Identity

Out of the idea of continuity with which the last chapter ended arises what is perhaps the single most important concept underlying all our thought on whatever subject, the concept of personal identity. In this chapter I shall consider the relation between personal identity and memory. It is a well-worn topic. I make no apology for treating it briefly, though it has been central to philosophy for centuries, and has never been more thoroughly considered than today. My aim is not to attempt to offer a new analysis of the idea of a person, nor of what counts as a single and continuing person. It is rather to connect the concept in its general employment with the value we attach to memory.

We have to consider two items, 'person' and 'identity'. It must be emphasized at the beginning that the concept 'person' is not a scientific concept. It does not fit into a list containing items such as 'fish' or 'bird'. It has no place in a list containing 'mammal' or 'marsupial'. It is what Roger Scruton (*Sexual Desire*, London, Weidenfeld and Nicolson, 1986) has called a 'superficial' concept. By this he means that, whatever the origin of the idea, it is one that now necessarily features in our ordinary thinking, and is a part, not of any analysis of the world, but of the life we actually lead. The plural of the word 'person' is, in ordinary use, 'people'. In the 1980s there has grown up a peculiar, partly sanctimonious, emphasis placed on the word 'people' almost every time that it is uttered. This emphasis calls attention to a value we ascribe. We are taught, for example, to refer not to 'the disabled' but to '*people* with disabilities'; we are told that politics (or, as it might be, education, or economics, or religion) is 'about people'. Each one of these people is a person, and each is both a person for others to treat as such, and a person for himself. He can think of himself from a 'first-person' standpoint. He is familiar with his own feelings, wishes, wants and aspirations. He has an inner life. The value-element in the idea of a person is primary; and this is all we need to bear in mind, by way of introduction.

Let us, also in an introductory way, now consider 'identity'. If we raise any question about the identity of an object, we must be referring to what are, or may be, in some sense, two or more objects. Thus if we ask whether a particular table is *the same*, we must mean the same *as* something; for instance the same as the one I wrote at last year, or the same as the one my mother brought back from the auction room forty years ago. Of course we use the expression 'the same' in other ways as well. It often means 'same kind' or 'same make'. So I can properly ask whether you have the same viburnum as I have in your garden, or the same car in your garage as mine. But, on the other hand, we may want to raise the question whether the thing before us, the table, is the very same identical individual object as another. As *what* other, then? If the answer is that the table *is* the same, there is no *other* for it to be the same as. There is only one thing in question, as our answer makes clear. Yet the question makes sense; for there are, after all, two things, a past-thing and a present-thing, a historical table, and a table at which we now sit and write. What we are identifying is the historical table, which features, say, in the story of the auction, with the table before which my chair is now drawn up. There is no sense at all in the identity-question, or the answer to it, unless we think of persistence through time, the past and present being *separate*.

Bergson, as we saw in chapter 2, held that we properly answer questions of identity, not in terms of persistence through time, but of the occupancy of space. Two things occupy two different spaces, one thing occupies only one space. He held that we identify temporal items (the bird I saw yesterday with the bird I can see today) only by making them quasi-spatial, laying them out end-to-end before our inner eye and counting them. In his view, as we saw, the true view of time is that which avoids the spatial metaphor, and which refuses to treat things as if they had hard, discernible edges, such as entails that they could be put side-by-side, or end-to-end. To common sense, however, his theory is implausible. Indeed, it seems somehow back to front. It is the essential characteristic of material objects, tables and chairs, that they can be moved about in space. One single object can be in many places; but not all at once. And so we have no possible means of identifying a table as the same table without the notion of temporal duration, surviving many changes of place. The notion of identity or non-identity is meaningless to common sense unless it means identity or multiplicity over a period of time.

However, in order to say that the table I am writing at is the same as the one I wrote at last year, we do not demand that it should be the same in every particular. It may have become scratched with the passage of time; its broken leg may have been repaired. These changes do not require us to say that there are two tables in question, not one. All that is necessary, for us to be able to claim that it is the same table, is a continuous *story* that can be told of how the table as it was last year came to be where it is now, in the shape it is now in.

It may be objected that by taking the example of a table, I have pre-judged the issue. For tables are, notoriously, physical objects able to be moved about from one spatial location to another. To speak of their identity may then indeed require the notion of temporal continuity through spatial change. But what of less spatially deter-mined objects? In their case, could there not be a concept of identity not temporal at all, but purely qualitative? Suppose, for example, that you and I have the same thought. We are both wondering how to fit everything we need into our two suitcases. It suddenly strikes us both that there is a third suitcase we could use in the basement. It does not matter whether we articulate this thought or not. Perhaps we both set off for the basement to locate the third case. The identity of the thought is, either way, guaranteed by its identical content. However, in this instance, the identity still depends on spatio-temporal continuity. For the referent of our thoughts is the same thing, namely the suitcase in the basement. In this instance, then, the identity of the thought, though not itself spatio-temporal, is defined in terms of an identical spatio-temporal object, the suitcase in the basement.

However, we could think of a different example. Suppose you are sitting next to someone at school lunch, and there is, beside you, a jug of treacle to pour over your suet pudding. Your neighbour says, 'Isn't treacle remarkably like lubrication oil?'; and you say, 'I had the same thought.' The proposition which identifies the two thoughts is, in this case, perfectly general. It may have been provoked by the sight of the treacle in the jug, but it refers not only to that treacle, but to treacle in general, treacle as a kind of stuff, and likewise to lubrication oil. It is, in its modest way, a timeless and universal thought, the same for all eternity. It looks at first as if the identity of the thought in such a case is quite independent of any spatio-temporal aspect of its content. It must be a matter of qualitative identity only. If there is no difference to be found between the content of the one thought and the other, then they must count as the same.

Now it has been suggested that if two people (apparently two, that is) had all and only the same thoughts in this sense, they would not be two people but one. I do not believe that this, even if possible to imagine, is at all plausible, according to the useful, 'superficial' view of people. For suppose that the apparently two people were classical scholars, musicologists or logicians. Is it not conceivable, even likely, that they might fall into dispute, even if all their thoughts were identical, about whose thoughts they actually were? For as long as these people were apparently two, they would have two names, and honours might be showered on one rather than on the other. The notion of 'same thought' is, not unexpectedly, ambiguous. In one sense it may mean thoughts with the same content, whether this content is identified by spatio-temporal considerations or by qualitative considerations alone. But, in another, perfectly familiar and useful sense, thoughts are not the same if I had one of them and you had the other. In this sense two thoughts may be the same thought only if we can forget their personal origin. Thus, if we found two ancient inscriptions, their authorship long forgotten, which expressed the same sentiment, though separated, perhaps by many years and many miles, we might, being struck by the fact, say that their content was indeed the same. But where authorship is in question, personal identity is stronger than identity of content. My thought is mine, and yours is yours. They are two thoughts (and the dispute may be about which came first). Qualitative similarity, however striking, is not, in such a case, sufficient to entitle us to claim identity.

If personal identity, then, has priority over identity of thought-content, we must try to find out what makes us say that there is one person, what leads us on the other hand to say that there are *two* people or more. Identity of thought-content will not be enough. And here, at the superficial level, we shall find that the case of people does not differ very much from that of the tables with which the chapter began. In order to make sense of the question 'Is it the same person?' we need to think, just as we did with the tables, of continuity through time. If I am to say 'This is the same person as the person who broke into my house last week', neither the likeness of the person before me to the one who broke in, nor differences between them are by themselves enough to settle the question. We need, besides likenesses, to be able to fill in a continuous physical history, linking the person then with the person now, the remembered with the now visible person.

Just as in the case of the identity of the table, a statement of identity with regard to a person contains at least the implication of a tense: 'He is the same as he *was*' or 'I am the same as I *was*.' (For questions about personal identity may be answered either from the outside, as when I identify the man before me as the housebreaker, or from within, as when I identify myself with the person who sat at the table last year.) In either case, there is a necessary reference to time past. Continuity of history is the central notion. If we think, then, of my identifying myself with the person I was, we are inevitably led to the connections between such identifications and memory. These connections have been variously explored by philosophers.

Locke (*Essay Concerning Human Understanding*, Book II, Chapter 27, Section 9) stated his criterion for personal identity in a way that immediately obliges us to think of the matter from within, from the standpoint of an 'I' reflecting on myself. 'To find wherein personal identity consists', he writes, 'we must consider what *person* stands for; which I think is a thinking intelligent being, that has reason and reflection, and can consider itself as itself, the same thinking thing, in different times and places.' So far so good, and few later philosophers have added to, or much altered, Locke's definition of a person, the kind of 'person' who features in our valued 'inter-personal relations'. But he continues more controversially. For he says that people are able to think of themselves as themselves only 'by that consciousness which is inseparable from thinking, and as it seems to me inseparable from it; it being impossible for anyone to perceive without perceiving that he does so'. According to this definition, then, if a creature perceived, but did not have present consciousness that he was perceiving, whatever that creature was he would not be a person. Locke goes on 'As far as consciousness can be extended backwards to any past action, so far reaches the identity of that person; it is the same self now as it was then; and it is by the same self with this present one that now reflects on it that that action was done.'

Locke insists that the concept of personal identity consists wholly in this continuity of consciousness. As far as the idea of 'same person' goes, he is not interested in any question about whether a man's body was composed of exactly the same material particles in the past as it is composed of now; nor is he even interested in the question whether there is or is not some continuing 'thinking substance' in the body, but distinct from it, and remaining the same through time.

For it is by the consciousness it has of its present thoughts and actions that it is *self to itself* now, and so will be the same self as far as the same consciousness can extend to actions past or to come; and would be by distance of time or change of substance no more two persons than a man be two men by wearing other clothes today than he did yesterday, with a long or short sleep between, the same consciousness uniting those distant actions into the same person whatever substances contributed to their productivity. (Section 10)

Locke distinguishes between the concept 'same person' and that of 'same man'; the former dependent wholly upon the extended consciousness or self-consciousness, the latter on bodily continuity. In this respect, 'same man' is no different from 'same armchair' or 'same butterfly', provided the latter does not mean 'same kind of butterfly'. This entails that if a man has radically changed in his appearance and capabilities between the time when he is eighteen and when he is eighty, he may know that he is the same person in 1980 as he was in 1918, but other people who have no access to his 'extended consciousness' may deem him to be a different man. 'For should the soul of a prince', Locke writes, 'carrying with it the consciousness of the prince's past life, enter and inform the body of a cobbler as soon as deserted by his own soul, everyone sees he would be the same person as the prince, accountable only for the prince's actions; but who would say it was the same man? . . . he would be the same cobbler to everyone besides himself.' (Section 15)

'Person' is, according to Locke, 'a forensic term'. It is the term, that is to say, by which responsibility is attributed both for past and for future actions, to a man, that is to a physical body. The physical body may change and the person remain the same; and Locke asks us to imagine, in the case of the prince and the cobbler, that the same consciousness could go with two totally different bodies (though not, in his imagined example, inhabiting two different bodies at the same time). The test is whether consciousness extends over the two bodies, so that the new cobbler is prepared, because of this consciousness, to take responsibility for what the prince did in his lifetime, and say, 'I did it'. If the cobbler says this, then we are entitled to speak of the cobbler and the prince as one and the same person. This example improbably stretches consciousness to cover qualitative differences, and differences of place. To cover differences in time is less of a problem. For obviously, to extend consciousness to cover differences of *time* is, generally, just another way of referring to memory.

Now in chapter 2 we saw that memory, in the sense of recollection, was taken by some philosophers to consist in a series of images, bearing the imprint of pastness upon them; while others thought of recollection as a unique kind of knowledge of the past. We can now take note of another feature which any truly recalling memory must have. It must contain the idea of self. Whether through images or through direct knowledge, to count as a memory a cognitive experience, or thought, must contain the conviction that I myself was the person involved in the remembered scene. The image, if there is one, must be labelled not only 'this belongs to the past' but also 'it belongs to *my* past'. The knowledge, if it is to be so described, must be knowledge that *I* had the earlier sensation or performed the earlier act. The knowledge is a kind of self-knowledge. It is in myself that the truth to be uncovered by recollection must lie.

There is a necessary connection, then, and one totally taken for granted in the non-philosophical world, between the concept of memory and that of the identical self, the person continuously existing through time. But there are difficulties. For it seems that we are involved in a circle. We would not be willing to call a thought a memory unless it involved the idea of the 'same self', the self now recollecting 'his' past. But equally we may have great sympathy with Locke's attempt to define the concept 'person' or 'same person' by reference to memory or extended consciousness. Which notion then, that of the person or that of memory, is to be given priority? Can one be said to be dependent on the other?

Before tackling the problem of circularity we must consider further Locke's notion of consciousness which gives rise to the problem. (A good discussion of this topic is to be found in 'Towards a Cognitive Theory of Consciousness', in Daniel Dennett, *Brain Storms*, Brighton, Harvester Press, 1981, pp. 149ff.) In the first place, it does not seem to be true that in perceiving or acting we have to be conscious at the time that we are perceiving or acting; or at least it is not necessary that we should know what we are perceiving or what we are doing. Nor is it true that being conscious, at the time, of what is happening is a condition of our having 'extended consciousness' or memory of it afterwards. To take one familiar example, I may remember clearly, and suddenly, that I have forgotten to do something (say, turn off the oven before I came out). I do not know what an accurate account of this phenomenon would be. But it is certain that Locke's 'extended consciousness' would not fit it, because if I had been conscious at the time that I was not switching off the oven, I would have immediately switched it off. Yet not only may I be quite sure afterwards that I failed to switch it off, but I would be quite willing to accept responsibility for my failure, though I was unconscious of it at the time.

Locke said that the term 'person' was a forensic term, by which we ascribe to a man responsibility for his past actions, and indeed for his undertakings with regard to the future which we presume he will be able to recollect. The implication is that if a man cannot remember what he did, if his consciousness cannot extend backwards to cover the act, he cannot be held responsible for it. This may, in certain cases, come near the truth. If, in order to be properly found guilty, a man must have acted with 'guilty intent', what are we to say of him if he was not then, and is not now, 'conscious' of his act? If a man is accused of a crime and seems sincerely to claim to remember nothing about it, his responsibility for it may be called in question, even if we know that he committed the crime. Nevertheless in ordinary domestic circumstances when we catch ourselves out in forgetfulness, we are ready, as a rule, and regretfully, to take responsibility for what we have done or failed to do, provided that external evidence is strong enough to show that no one else can possibly be blamed. Perhaps it is a matter of degree. If we reach extremes of forgetfulness, so that whole areas of our lives are systematically lost to us, as in the notorious cases of 'split personality' (see, for example, *Eve*, by Chris Costner Sizemore and Ellen Sain Pittillo, London, Pan Books, 1970) then it is very unlikely that we will feel responsibility for the forgotten acts of the 'other personality'.

At the same time we cannot hold that personal identity depends exclusively on that which we remember, still less on that which we were fully aware of at the time, and could then describe. Many of our memories, after all, and those we most readily embrace as our own, are of scenes which, at the time, were a mere background to the action, hardly noticed at all. How conscious is a child of the buildings, the fields, the gardens, the smells, the clouds under the influence of which he plays? Yet he can later not only recognize them as familiar but may increasingly recall them in detail, as he grows older. On some theories of the personality, the most important factor is the memory of things which no one could say the person was conscious of at the time, such as the trauma of birth. Such theories may indeed involve an undue extension of the idea of memory; nevertheless that they are even partly intelligible implies that we do not really believe that we need to have been fully aware of an event for it to be recalled at a later time.

Locke's notion of 'consciousness' is, then, unsatisfactory; and so perhaps is his derivation of the idea of 'same person' from the idea of extended consciousness or memory. Bishop Butler (*First Dissertation to the Analogy of Religion*) criticized him, both on the grounds that he demanded consciousness of our acts for them to be ours, and on the grounds that he gave priority to the idea of memory over that of myself. Bishop Butler wrote:

Though consciousness of what is past does ascertain our personal identity to ourselves yet to say that it makes personal identity, or is necessary to our being the same persons, is to say that a person has not existed a single moment nor done one action but what he can remember; indeed done nothing but what he reflect upon. And one should really think it self-evident, that consciousness of personal identity presupposes and therefore cannot constitute personal identity, any more than knowledge, in any other case, can constitute truth, which it presupposes.

A genuine memory of the past is intuitively acceptable, as knowledge, to the person who remembers (though he may also accept things he doesn't 'really' remember). How can this be so unless the notion of 'I', to whom the past belongs, is already given? How can the concept of 'I', to whom that past belongs, depend on memory for its existence? Must it not be logically prior to the concept of memory itself?

Many philosophers and psychologists have, like Bishop Butler, reversed Locke's priorities. William James (*Principles of Psychology*, London, 1890, Vol. I, chapters on Self and Memory) defines memory as follows: 'Memory proper is the knowledge of a former state of mind after it has already dropped from the consciousness; or rather it is the knowledge of an event or fact of which, meantime, we have not been thinking, with the added consciousness that we have thought or expressed it before.' This, as a definition of recalling, is treading familiar ground. But he goes on to say that, in order to identify memory as memory and not mere imagination, the thought, or fact thought of, must be expressly dated in the past; and the past of which it forms part must be *my* past. It must possess a certain 'warmth and intimacy' which, he says, characterizes any experience appropriated by someone as *his own*. I am supposed to think of my past, that is, as I might think of my bed or my clothes, objects possessed by me, familiar, comfortable, my belongings. James is unwilling to allow, indeed, that there is any such 'consciousness' of the present as Locke's account demands. He is inclined to argue that what happens to me now, at a precise moment, is not 'mine' till afterwards: 'All the intellectual value to us of a state of mind depends on our after-memory of it. Only then is it combined in a system and knowingly made to contribute to a result. Only then does it *count* for us. So the effective consciousness we have of our states is the after-consciousness.' (op. cit.) Thus, what happens to me can be *turned into* one of my belongings; but it is the concept of myself as the recipient and possessor, the systematic organizer of experiences, that is central. Memory could neither exist, nor be valued, if this centre of experience, the familiar self, did not exist.

Sartre (*Being and Nothingness*, pp. 112ff.) is as certain as William James and Bishop Butler that the idea of the self is the essential prerequisite of memory, in the sense of recollection. Indeed he argues that it is the prerequisite of the very notion of 'the past'. 'The past', he writes, 'is characterized as the past of something or somebody; one *has* a past . . . there is not first a universal past which is later particularized into concrete pasts. On the contrary, it is particular pasts that we discover first.' He argues that the notion of myself as the recipient, the one who 'has' experience, is itself given in the immediate consciousness that I have of 'my' experiences. He refers to my awareness that I am a thinking, experiencing being as 'the pre-reflective *cogito*', and it is present in all experience. It is a vague, undifferentiated awareness of self accompanying all perceptions and all sensations. But his 'pre-reflective *cogito*' is in one important respect unlike Descartes's *cogito*. For it makes me present to myself, not only as a thinking being as Descartes supposed, but as one that is embodied. Sartre sometimes speaks of 'a persistent bitter taste, a permanent nausea, which is the presence of my body to myself', or of 'a dull and inescapable nausea perpetually revealing my body to myself'. Such an awareness of self, part 'mental' and part 'physical', is what sets apart humans ('beings-for-themselves', in the phrase he borrowed from Hegel) from all other things.

For, in Sartre's view, this human awareness of self is identical with a certain distancing from experience. A tree or a typewriter is simply that; it is completely that which it can be described as being. Even if we happen not to know everything about it, in principle we could know everything. And we could also predict, in principle, everything that will happen to it. We can regard these non-human things wholly scientifically, and discover the laws which determine what will happen tomorrow, after the events of today. The rain, the sun and the greenfly of yesterday determine the growth of my rose today. They make the rose what it is.

In the case of humans, on the other hand, since they reflect on what they are, there is room for them to determine what they will be, in accordance with the interpretation they place upon what has happened to them. The past becomes 'their' past precisely because it is the subject of reflection. Although I cannot change the past, I can change my view of it, and the use I put it to. It is like a tool made in a certain shape, but flexible, and thus able to be adapted to new circumstances. And thus, Sartre concludes, my past is me.

Perhaps it would be better to say that my past is my life, and my life is continuous, with a future as well as with a past. What my future will be is a matter of choice, but a choice that cannot be made except in the light of the past. The things I have to choose between would not be as they are if my past had been different. My consciousness of myself in the present, as a person with choices to make, is a consciousness inseparable from what has happened to me. My present cannot be divorced from my past, neither can my concept of self be separated from my awareness of what I was in the past. The person and 'his' past are one and the same.

The injunction of Solon to 'call no man happy until he is dead' is interpreted by Sartre, as indeed it was by Aristotle, to mean that a man is to be described in terms of his life. Therefore what sort of a man he is cannot be fully described until the moment comes when he has had his life. He is his whole life, and that means he is his past. 'My' past means the past I carry round with me as I live my life, in memory.

The great advantage of such a view over Locke's is that my memory is not confined by it to that which I can deliberately call to mind, nor to that which I deliberately recall, having been fully aware of it at the time. It is a view both more realistic, and more comformable to what we know to be true of memory than the theory of Locke or, for that matter, of Norman Malcolm (see chapter 3 above).

Moreover, if Sartre is right there is little point in pursuing questions of priority between the notions of memory and self. We are, after all, perfectly accustomed to pairs or groups of ideas so related to each other that it is impossible to conceive one without the other, and where a speaker could hardly be supposed to understand the one without having some understanding of the other. In such cases it is probably a matter simply of individual chance which idea first became familiar to us: which word first entered our vocabulary. There is no answer to the question which 'has priority', the lines or the angles of a triangle; nor of which 'comes first', uphill or downhill; whether we are first acquainted with the idea of an orchestra, and then of individual instruments that make it up, or the other way about. The notions are truly interdependent. There is no reason, then, why we should choose between Locke, on the one hand, and Bishop Butler and William James on the other. It is more fruitful to follow the Sartrean route along which we discover the concept of memory and personal identity to be logically interlocked, neither separable from the other.

Nevertheless, we may still find ourselves faced with a question, and one which Sartre never explicitly raised, though his answer is implied. Memory would generally be thought of as a 'mental' phenomenon, something 'in the mind'. Are we to believe, then, that personal identity, interwoven as it is with memory, is also a 'mental' phenomenon? Is it the case that if someone is the same person as he was five years ago, he must primarily display 'mental continuity' over time? This kind of question has greatly exercised philosophers, particularly in the twentieth century. Even if it is agreed that 'memory' and 'person' or 'self' must be connected, we still have not settled what exactly are the criteria for the identity of persons. How do we actually decide whether a person is the same over a period of time? And if we do not know how to settle this crucial question, how can we be thought to understand what a person *is*? For if I have no idea how I would settle the question whether what I heard today is the same symphony as I heard yesterday, it cannot really be that I know what a symphony is. If I know what a symphony is, I at least know what would have to be true if I could be said to have heard the same symphony twice. It does not matter that I will sometimes get the identification wrong. Similarly, if I know what a person is, then I will know what would have to be true if the person before me was to be the same as the person I met five years ago, even if, in practice, I might be deceived or otherwise mistaken. We shall expect that the criteria for the identity of persons over time will contain some reference to memory; but there may be other criteria as well. And among all the criteria, which is the most important? Perhaps memory, our chief concern, is the *least* important?

The difficulties presented by such questions are notorious. Part of the trouble is that common sense, without which philosophy is pointless, rejects the very formulation of the question. For suppose we ask 'How do I know that I am the same person as I was forty years ago?': common sense suggests that this must be a futile question since it already contains its own answer. The first person pronoun, 'I', is always used, if used in one sentence, to refer to the *same identical person*. If two people were even possibly involved in the forty-year period, the question would be differently expressed. But it is very difficult to see how to express *that* question differently. Let us try some possible questions: (1) 'Am I the same person as the person who bore my name forty years ago?'; (2) 'Am I the same person as the person who wrote the review with my name at the end?'; (3) 'Am I the same person as the person who used to wear these baby clothes?' We would, it seems, have to take different steps to provide answers to these different questions.

The first, as it stands, is too vague to be intelligible. Although questions about the identity of persons often, in practice, arise because of the identity of names, we know very well that more than one person may bear the same name. In order to get this sort of difficulty out of the way, we need to be much more specific about the then bearer of my name, and also to give some context within which the question could be asked. Suppose that I am presented with a schoolgirl's essay, with a date and my name on it. Then immediately the question whether the person who bore my name and wrote the essay on the date given at the top of the page was in fact I, makes perfect sense. We can put it more simply. *Did I write that essay?* If 'it all comes back to me', then we shall be happy to say that I did. And this, of course, is the strength of Locke's position. But it may not 'come back to me'; and in that case, if the question has to be answered, then I shall have to look for external evidence. If, for example, the essay has been found at the back of the desk I have always used since I was at school, or among other papers indisputably mine, then circumstantial evidence will be enough. I shall say '*I must have written it.*'

The second question (whether I am the person who signed the review) seems rather different. The problem might, it is true, be whether there is someone else of the same name writing reviews for the same paper as I write for. But it might be that I was asking whether I or someone else, purporting to be me, wrote the review. In this case it would, as a matter of fact, be unlikely that I would use the word 'same' in my question. 'Did *I* write that review?' is more likely to be expanded into 'Did I *or someone else* write that review?' Suppose that I remember nothing about it, though the review is only a few weeks old. Then it is likely that I shall conclude that I didn't write it, unless I am notoriously, almost pathologically, forgetful. The longer ago the review was written, the more it approximates to the schoolgirl essay, and the more reliance we shall be inclined to place on circumstantial evidence, rather than memory, to settle the question of authorship.

When we come to the third question 'Am I the same person who wore these baby clothes?', circumstantial evidence will probably have to settle the question, by itself. It is not to be expected that I would remember wearing the baby clothes, even if it can be proved that they were in some sense mine. That they were mine and that I wore them will simply be a fact to be accepted, as I might accept the fact that the baby's shoe you show me was worn by your eldest son, though I never knew him in those days. It is a matter of history. In order to establish that I wore the clothes, we need to spend more ingenuity on establishing the continuous historical existence of the clothes than on establishing anything about the continuous exist- ence of me as a person.

There are two related points especially to be noticed here. Although the examples support Locke's contention up to a point, in that *if* I remember doing the thing in question it would probably be accepted that I was the person who did it, the converse does not hold. That I do not remember doing something is conclusive evi- dence that I did not do it only if certain conditions are fulfilled. The thing done must have been relatively important, it must have been relatively close in time to the question raised about it; and I must be supposed to have an ordinarily reliable memory. None of these conditions is exactly specifiable; all rely on some sort of conception of the normal. But all are intelligible in practice. And, as we shall see presently, the fact that there is an implicit appeal to normality in such cases is itself significant.

If the event in question was very long ago, or if I am known to be unusually forgetful, or if the thing in question was very trivial, then that I cannot remember doing it is not taken to entail that the person who did it was not I. There are, in principle, ways of establishing my identity or non-identity with the person who did it, other than my memory. There is, for example, the memory of other people. There may be written records, diaries, newspaper accounts, reports of criminal trials and so on. All such evidence can be described as historical or external. There is an inescapable sense in which I cannot refuse to acknowledge that I did something, if it can be established by external evidence *that* I did it, whether I can remember doing it or not (though there may be circumstances in which I can refuse to *take responsibility* for what I did and where responsibility would not be laid on me, see p. 60).

What does it mean, then, to say that it can be established that I was the person who did something, if I have no recollection of doing it? The answer is very simple. The person who did the thing must be shown to be identical with me in the sense that *if* someone else had had their eye on that person from the moment when she was doing the thing in question until now, there would have been no *different* person involved; only one agent, who is I. The hypothetical spy, watching the original act, and also confronting me now, would be able in principle to fill up *all the temporal gaps* between now and then, and would in principle be able to say, 'No one else came along. No one took her place.'

The *continuity* thus established is the continuity of a spatial object, which can move and change, but yet be said to be the same. Identifying me with the baby who wore the baby clothes all those years ago is no different in principle from identifying the clothes themselves, when we find them in a box, with the clothes worn at my christening. The clothes have been moved from one house to another, put in one chest of drawers and then another, have yellowed with age, become ragged. But in their history, there has been no time when anyone actually destroyed them and said 'let's get a new set of clothes'. We make this kind of identification of objects through time extremely frequently, and of course we don't in fact have to keep our eye on an object throughout its history in order to identify and re-identify it with itself. I can say 'That is the same cat that my daughter brought from Devonshire in a basket when he was a kitten', and I certainly have not watched my cat without remission for ten years. But I have seen him often, have noticed how he has grown and changed, in ways expected of cats, and I know that he has never been lost, he has not died, I have never said, 'We must replace him with another cat.'

The point is that, though obviously we sometimes wrongly identify things over time, yet on the whole, and in normal circumstances, we can do it with confidence. Our confidence is greater, the more we know about the *kind* of thing in question. I know how kittens turn into cats, babies into grown-ups, bright new copies of books into dog-eared old ones, caterpillars into butterflies, soggy uncooked cakes into light and risen ones, and so on. Someone ignorant of cooking might not believe that the cake he was eating was the same as the cake I put into the oven half an hour before, because it looks and smells different; I know better. Someone ignorant of humans might deny that I could ever have fitted into the christening clothes. But humans know better.

Notoriously, there are objects (including humans) of which gradually all the parts wear out and are replaced by others. Such gradual replacement does not prevent our saying that the object is the same through time. Normally, we think that there have been two objects (or more than two) whenever a *whole new object* has replaced the old. I may be very proud of the fact that I have kept the same bicycle ever since I was fifteen years old. Every bit of the bicycle may at one time or another have been replaced, but there has never been a day when I said, 'I must, after all, get a new bicycle.' I have never bought a whole bicycle, only new bits for the old one.

If I identify someone, then, with the person who, years ago, pushed me into the sea, even though he has no recollection of doing so, I identify him by my access to his history as a physical object, however much he has changed over the years. It is more difficult to make such an identification than it is to identify my desk as the one I used ten years ago, because people move about more than desks, and change in more complicated ways. But the principle is the same. Locke would say that what is identified here is the same *man*, not the same *person*. I am arguing that his distinction is a confusing and mistaken one.

It might be argued that our original question, 'Am I the same person as I was forty years ago?', although it seems in some way to contain its own answer by its use of the first-person pronoun, can be understood, and may be quite seriously raised. If, between different phases of a person's life, he changes radically, not in the predictable physiological ways but in all his tastes and habits; if his experiences greatly enlighten or embitter him; if he was once in love with someone he later despises, such changes may make him say that he is a different person now. Proust, one of the novelists most pro-foundly concerned with questions of identity, was aware of the fragmentary nature of persons over time. Marcel in love is not the same as Marcel not in love, nor can he think of himself as the precursor of the person he will be when he is no longer in love. He cannot identify himself with the person he was as a child (any more than he can with his future self), through any mechanical or intellectual devices such as calling up visual images of the past. For such images might just as well, if deliberately thought up, refer to someone else, not himself. Proust would deny the essential differ-ence between the images of the two men discussed by Ryle, one of whom had, and the other of whom had not, been part of a naval engagement. Insofar as both men deliberately form images of the engagement, their images will tell them nothing. For what memory of this kind produces, according to Proust, is 'snapshots'; and a snapshot does not carry its own reference as an identifying mark upon it. (See, for example, Proust, *Time Regained*, translated by Stephen Hudson, London, Chatto and Windus, 1944, p. 211.)

We may readily agree with Proust that it is difficult, if not impossible, fully to associate ourselves with those future persons who do not yet exist. It is now, let us say, unimaginable that there will be a person who is identical with me and who yet is indifferent to an object which now obsesses me, and this although experience tells me that my crazes and passions pass after a time. Present obsession simply is the state of feeling as if there could never be a world which did not contain me in the grip of the feeling I now have. Equally, if I am very angry, and, as I think, with just cause, it is impossible to identify myself with the person who will, tomorrow, have forgotten all about it. If I could identify myself with the future, I should not be really angry in the present. As I now tear about the house, it is hard for me to identify with the old lady who will, perhaps, one day hobble slowly about it on a stick. I know nothing of what such a person will be like.

With the past, however, it is different (and Proust, for all his belief in fragmentation, knew that it was). The past self in some sense exists for me even if I cannot at the moment remember exactly what that self did or felt. The past self can be revived. There is always the possibility of *feeling* the identity between myself now and myself then. And this is so because it can be shown, conclusively, that the past self was, physically, the person I now am. There would be no interest in the past self if the physical identity were not given, if the very same human being were not assumed as part of the same story.

The case of identifying myself over time therefore is really no different from the case of identifying someone else as the same person over time. I have, let us say, a cross and miserable child, whining, tired, pale, always discontented, unable to concentrate. I take him to hospital, I see him into the operating theatre, I see him come out, his tonsils removed. Eventually I take him home and he gets better. Gradually his character and his appearance and his habits all change. He is energetic, happy, cheerful, able to concentrate. He is, I say, a different child. But the point is I know he is not. If I thought that I had literally received a different child out of the operating theatre from the one I left at the door (which is, after all, a theoretical possibility), I should be frantic. However awful he is, one can't just throw away one's child and get another. I know that this child is the same as the old one, only better. Surgery has improved him. Just so I may take my bicycle to the shop and get a thorough job done on it which improves it, I may say, 'beyond all recognition'. But I do recognize it all the same. It is not a new bicycle.

The over-riding criterion for sameness of persons, then, in the common sense view, is *physical continuity of body over time*. It is the same as the criterion we use for sameness of bicycles, cats or tables. If we speak otherwise, we speak in metaphors. 'I am a new woman'; I could not say this if it were true. And that our bodily identity over time feels complex; that it is confirmed by the inner knowledge of our past which memory brings, should not in the least surprise us, if we reflect that memory itself is necessarily connected with, and a part of, the brains and bodies that we have. If memory of the past is, as I have argued in the previous chapter, *caused* by what has happened to us, that is to our bodies and our brains, it is no surprise that the continuity over time of those bodies should, at least sometimes, be confirmed by memory-knowledge.

For common sense, memory is an extra dimension, available to 'beings-for-themselves', or conscious beings, unavailable to bicycles or tables, but making no substantial difference to the question of identity. And this ought to be all there is to say on the subject. For the mental aspects of a person cannot be separated from the physical aspects. The mind is not another thing to be considered separately from the body. In the typical or normal case of a man, the man is a person who remembers things that have happened to him, not all of them, it is true, and he may be puzzled as to why he remembers some things and not others; but, often, he does remember. Then he can quite happily say, if required, 'I am the person who locked the door when I left the house', or even 'I am the person who suffered concussion and can remember nothing of the accident.' The normal person can use the general and historical criteria of bodily continuity in his own case, whether or not he can use the Locke-like criterion of 'consciousness' in a continuous way. We do not need to answer the question whether personal identity is primarily 'mental'. Like memory itself, it is mental *and* physical.

But there is a peculiar fascination in the question of what would happen if my memories were taken over by someone else, in part or in whole. Locke's fantasy of the prince and the cobbler has not died. It has recently been revitalized by questions turning on the transplanting of brains (if kidneys and hearts can be transplanted why not brains?). For many philosophers, the intrinsic feasibility or otherwise of such procedures is of little importance. From Locke to Wittgenstein and beyond they have tried to sort out conceptual tangles by imagining cases where the tangles would not occur, where the various strands which go to make up a concept (such as personal identity) are, in the imagination, artificially separated. So Locke separated the body from the consciousness of the prince and deemed that the identity of his person lay with his consciousness, and not with his body; and so the cobbler became the same person as the prince. The argument is this; just because memory and a continuously existing single body generally go together, we must not suppose that they are necessarily connected. Let us imagine them separate, and see what we would say.

The most widely discussed contemporary imagining is of a man, call him John, whose brain is divided between two other (brainless) bodies. The new bodies are supposed to have John's character, abilities and apparent memories, or at least some of these attributes each. Are we to say that John is identical with both the new men, or with one of them, or with neither? (See Parfitt, *Philosophical Review*, 1971). If I woke up in hospital one day with a new brain, donated by someone else, my old brain having been removed, would I become a new person? And if you, in the next bed, had half a brain of which I had the other half, both halves having once been John's, would you and I now be the same person? What would our joint relation be to John?

In the philosophical examples within which these questions are discussed, we are not told much about what is supposed to go along with the transplanted brain. Character is vaguely mentioned, and apparent memories. But it is not clear whether, for example, I am supposed to wake up knowing Greek, or how to play the Brahms violin concerto, which I did not know before; whether you wake up with an aversion to celery and a fear of spiders, which the donor had and you hadn't. But leaving these details aside, it is still perfectly clear that, according to the common sense view, the answer to the above questions must be that you and I are two different people, and that both of us are different from the donor, who is now no more. The fact that at the time when we regain consciousness we know some of the same things, answer questions about our pasts in the same way, both appearing to have forgotten much of what differentiated us before, must be seen by common sense to be a temporary confusion. We may indeed ourselves be muddled about who we are, and what our pasts have been. But the nurses and doctors will not be muddled. We shall have our operating theatre labels round our wrists, and that will be that. As soon as we begin to recover, it will presumably be the case that each of us will have different, though doubtless for a time similar, experiences. The nurse will spill the soup over you but not over me; my neighbour on my other side will die, yours will recover. Later we may be separated geographically, and begin to build up a new store of memories, which will further and further differentiate us, one from another. However creepily alike we may be in some ways, we shall be two, just as identical twins are two people, not one. They may share their genes, but they cannot share their geography.

Now Parfitt, in the article mentioned above, has argued that it does not really matter how we decide to answer the questions about the identity of the three people in the story, the donor and the two recipients of his brain. In fact it begins to make no sense to answer these questions in terms of identity at all. We ought instead to think, not of *continuity* of individuals through time, but of *survival* through time. Things can survive in bits and pieces. A thriving plant can be divided up, and bits of it given round to the neighbours. All or some may survive. We are not interested in asking whether these new plants are identical with the old. Identity, Parfitt says, is a one/one relation holding between an individual at one time and an individual at a different time. Survival, on the other hand, can be a one/many relation between an individual at one time and any number of individuals at another time. If we accustomed ourselves to this idea, he argues, we should become less self-interested; less obsessed, that is, with the single continuing individual who is identically ourselves. For we should be able to think not just of ourselves in the future, but of all the people with whom we were, more or less, physiologically or psychologically connected. Survival, unlike identity, is a matter of degree.

Metaphorically, of course, such an idea is quite familiar. If a man has ten children, each of whom is genetically connected with himself, each of whom inherits some of his characteristics, it would not be too fanciful to say that more of him survives than would have survived had he had one child, or none. And if we want to strengthen the case for survival by inventing brain transplants, then we could indeed give a new sense to the expression 'He has his father's brain.' But it is a crucial part of my thesis that though the father, about to give his brain for his youngest child, might be glad to think that he was to survive in his children (indeed, he might be glad of this, whether or not he had to sacrifice his own brain in order to do so), this gladness or interest in the future would not be the same as an interest in *himself*. He thinks of his future *self* differently. Parfitt and those who have discussed his article have tended to obscure the difference between thinking about myself and thinking about those with whom I may be variously connected, by talking of what 'matters to us'. But different things matter to different people. It is certainly possible, and always has been, to interest ourselves in the future and not in ourselves as part of that future. Who otherwise would have gone in for landscape-gardening, that most altruistic of the arts? But that is not to suggest that such a diffuse interest in the future may be substituted for an interest in ourselves as individuals.

Parfitt, I think, confuses things still further by suggesting that we *ought* to make this substitution, and that if people in general thought in terms, not of individual identity, but of a spreading survival, it would somehow reduce the amount of bad self-interest in the world. I am more concerned in the present study, however, with what we *do* value than with what we *ought to* value, even if (as I do not) I thought Parfitt's plans for conceptual revision were feasible. My sole concern with the philosophical theories of personal identity has been to show how memory is interwoven with the concept of self. But since we do, as things are, feel deeply about our own identity over time, we, equally, value memory as part of this identity. Insofar as we value the one, we value the other. I am my body; but my body, including, of course, my brain, carries memory along with it, however patchy and incomplete my memory may be. No concept of bits of me surviving without memory, or of my memory surviving in someone else's body, even if such things could be properly imagined, would be a substitute for the profundity of my interest in identity, being the same person from birth, through all vicissitudes, till death. That some people, in some circumstances, through severe illness or amnesia, may lose this sense of their own identity, does not in the least contradict the proposition that in the ordinary case that sense of identity is what a continuing human being has, and wishes to preserve.

David Wiggins, in an article written for Amelie Rorty's collection, *The Identities of Persons* (University of California Press, 1976), has argued most persuasively, as it seems to me, that the idea of personal identity, that idea which Locke, among others, was trying to analyse, must be that of the identity over time of a living member of a natural kind. If we take this view, then, as I have suggested already, Locke was wrong to say that 'person' is a forensic term, insofar as this implies that it is *only* that. For this, in turn, implies that whether or not we choose to speak of x as the same person as y (who committed the crime) will be a matter of judgement or decision, perhaps a matter of convention. If we abandon Locke's distinction between 'person' and 'man', then we are entitled, as I have suggested, to treat the method of determining the continuous identity of a person through time as the same *kind* of method as that which we use to determine the continuous identity of a bicycle or a cat through time. But the cat is the better analogue. For she, the cat, is the same cat from birth to death. People equally are living members of a species, the species *Homo sapiens*. In establishing the identity of someone over time, then, we are establishing that he is the same member of the species and that he has been alive all the time, whatever his physical or mental condition.

There are, as we have seen, partial uses of the word 'same' as when I say 'I am not the same as I was when I was a baby', though I am actually the same. There may likewise be partial uses of the word 'person'. One may hear it said of a baby that he is 'a real person' now, or of someone who has suffered brain damage that he is no longer a person. But these are not central uses of the term. It is no use looking for criteria by which we can distinguish persons from non-persons, though, doubtless, such criteria could be used in certain circumstances. If we are interested in the identity of persons over time, then the physiological criteria we have discussed must over-ride all others. Wiggins ends his article thus:

> The hospitalized amnesiac or Nijinsky even at the last stage of madness are the same man and the same person . . . Let us amend Locke, and say a person is any animal, the physical make-up of whose species constitutes the species' typical members, thinking, intelligent beings, with reason and reflection, and typically enables them to consider themselves as themselves the same thinking things, in different times and places. Memory is not then irrelevant to personal identity, but the way it is relevant is simply that it is one highly important element among others in the account of what it is for a person to be still there, *alive*. It plays its part in determining the *continuity principle for persons*, as opposed to bodies or cadavers.

I agree with this conclusion. Memory, the highly important element in the account of what it is to be a person who is still there, *is that which is caused by his having been there, the same physiological system, over time*. We need to consider hypothetical transplants, if at all, only if they help us to identify the significance of memory in the normal, non-transplant case (just as we may consider cases of amnesia, if these throw light on the central role of memory for those who still retain it). We can accept that a powerful sense of, and interest in, his own identity, continuous through time, is a normal feature of the species man. This interest is necessarily and inextricably bound up with man's capacity for memory, and the pleasure in remembering that the species as a whole displays. In the next chapters we shall consider some of the characteristic forms that this capacity, and this pleasure, may take.

5

Memory into Art:
Paradise Regained

In the foregoing chapters it has been argued that memory and personal identity are inextricably linked, neither concept being prior to nor separable from the other. The sense of personal identity that each of us has is a sense of continuity through time. We could not have this without memory, in the full sense of recollection. For if memory were simply a matter of learning and not forgetting, though it would imply physical continuity, it would not necessarily speak to us of it. We might be able today to find our way through the maze, having learned to do so by repeated trials. This, of course, implies that we, our bodies, have been at the entrance to the maze before today. But unless we can recall at least some of our trials, we would know no more than that today we can find our way through the maze. We would not feel ourselves to be the very animals who learned, the hard way.

It scarcely needs saying that the sense of personal identity, and with it the idea of memory itself, is a central starting point for art, especially, but not exclusively, the art of the Romantic period. In this chapter I shall explore some of the ways in which writers have sought to transform memory into art. Just as we could divide philosophers into those who conceived of memory as essentially a matter of having certain images and those who, on the other hand, thought of memory as a special kind of knowledge, so writers may be similarly divided, a philosophical background partly explaining their assumptions, but not dictating the outcome of their thought.

Though the distinction just drawn is of considerable theoretical interest, and may even throw some light on what memory is actually like as we experience it, it has to be said that, whichever aspect of memory is chiefly emphasized, there are the closest possible links between it and imagination; indeed these two powers are impossible to separate. (We may recall that Sartre, in writing of the imagination, drew most of his examples of the image from the images of memory.) For, whether we are imagining or recalling, we are thinking of something that is not before our eyes and ears, and of something that has meaning for us, and may be imbued with strong emotions. We could say that, in recalling something, we are employing imagination; and that, in imagining something, exploring it imaginatively, we use memory. There can be no sharp distinction. Imagination, like memory itself, may be thought of either in terms of a kind of imagery, or as a kind of knowledge or understanding.

Those philosophers who concentrated on memory as essentially a matter of inner experience, the experience of an image, sought for a special character in the experienced image to distinguish a memory-image from one that was the free product of the imagination. We saw, in chapter 2, something of the difficulty they found in describing or identifying any such special 'feel'. But perhaps the notion introduced and considered in chapter 3 may help us here. For we there argued that, whatever its character, memory must be causally connected with the event to which it referred (nor did we find any need to invent a special sense of 'cause' to account for the admittedly mysteriously patchy and non-uniform relation between a witnessed event and its effect, the memory). It is true that we were, in chapter 3, particularly concerned with the causal relation between an event and a later claim to *know* about that event, with no necessary component of an image or inner experience to substantiate that claim. But it would be absurd to deny that images occur, or that they often accompany a claim to remember. Indeed, the occurrence of an image may often be that which immediately leads to the claim to knowledge. So if memory claims must, as we there argued, be causally related to that to which they refer, then so must memory images, where they exist. We take it for granted that a cause precedes its effect in time. It may therefore be that the 'feeling of pastness' sought by philosophers to mark off the memory image from other images, arises simply from the assumption we make that our present image has a particular *causal* history. I speak of an assumption, because, of course, we may be wrong about the history of a particular image. We may have acquired it through being told about an event, or we may, like Goethe, be in doubt about what the causal history of the image actually is.

If this suggestion is right, then neither 'pastness' nor 'familiarity' need be invoked as special recognizable characteristics of a certain class of images. It is rather that in calling (rightly or wrongly) certain images memory-images, we are claiming for them a particular causal background, which we spontaneously believe that they have.

Now this causal assumption may itself carry an emotional content. It may affect us in a particular way. The very fact that the cause precedes the effect, that the course of history cannot be reversed, nor time move backwards, may itself contribute to the sense of loss often so powerfully associated with the images of memory, both in literature and in life. Walter de la Mare (*Pleasures and Speculations*, London, Faber and Faber, 1940) spoke of W. H. Hudson, writing of his own memories, as appealing to 'the child in us, the lost or forsaken youth'. And there is no doubt that this lurking figure, the lost youth, informs many of our memories. But it is not only for our lost childhood that we yearn. Anything that is *over*, even though we may be thankful that it is, carries with it the possibility of yearning. We shall never *have* it again. It is a lost *possession*. No wonder that so many people believe that, if they could only preserve the past, whether in autobiography, by photographs, or by some other means, they would be happy. The past is a paradise from which we are necessarily excluded, and this is true even though, when it was present, it was less than paradisical. And so an image, if it is taken to be a memory-image, may convey a sense of joy, in the regaining of something thought to be lost for ever.

The thought that 'time past shall never come again' is as old as literature itself, as is the celebration of a partial recovery of past time in images. We may start, however, with an exceptionally clear and comparatively recent description of the nature of the memory-image itself, to be found in the work of W. H. Hudson referred to by Walter de la Mare. It comes from the first chapter of his autobiography (*Far Away and Long Ago: a History of my Early Life*, London, Everyman, 1939). I am not concerned here with the fact that he was writing autobiography. I shall have more to say on that particular form of literature in chapter 6. My interest for the time being is simply in what he tells us about the *form* of his recollection. He is explaining how he came to write the book, starting it during the course of an illness (op. cit., p. 1ff.):

On the second day of my illness, during an interval of comparative ease, I fell into recollections of my childhood, and at once I had that far, that forgotten past, with me again as I had never previously had it. It was not like that mental condition known to most persons when some sight or sound or, more frequently, the perfume of some flower, associated with our early life, restores the past suddenly and so vividly that it is almost an illusion. That is an intensely emotional condition, and vanishes as quickly as it comes. This was different . . . it was as if the cloud shadows and haze had passed away and the entire wide prospect beneath me made entirely visible. Over it all my eyes could range at will, choosing this or that point to dwell upon, to examine it in all its details. What a happiness it would be, I thought, in spite of discomfort and pain and danger, if this vision would continue . . . It was to me a marvellous experience; to be here, propped up with pillows in a dimly lighted room, the night-nurse idly dozing by the fire; the sound of the everlasting wind in my ears, howling and dashing the rain against the window panes; to be aware of all this, feverish and ill and sore, conscious of my danger too, and at the same time to be thousands of miles away, out in the sun and wind, rejoicing in other sights and sounds, happy again with that ancient and long-lost and now recovered happiness.

The completeness of the images, the fact that he could examine them at will, spending time exploring each, suggested to Hudson that 'nothing is ever blotted out'. Everything we have ever experienced is somehow 'stored' but only in exceptional circumstances will it ever be retrieved. The retrieval, when it does occur, is itself a rare pleasure and unique excitement.

The most serious and the best-known theory of the place of the memory-image in literary art dates from more than a hundred years before Hudson wrote those words in 1918. It is to be found in Wordsworth's 1798 poems, in parts of *The Prelude*, and in the 1802 version of the *Preface to the Lyrical Ballads*. In Wordsworth we can trace quite clearly both the belief in the memory-image as the central form of recollection, and also the significance of recollection itself, its crucial importance to us as a source both of meaning and of truth.

Though Wordsworth, as certainly as W. H. Hudson, describes the act of recollecting as the contemplation of images, the concept of the image itself is not straightforward in his case. It is hung about with the trappings of philosophical history. I have argued elsewhere (*Imagination*, Mary Warnock, London, Faber and Faber, 1976) following the suggestion of C. C. Clarke (*Romantic Paradox*, London, Routledge and Kegan Paul, 1962) that, lying behind Wordsworth's theory of poetry as well as his practice, and behind the vocabulary in which he described recollection, was the philosophical tradition of Locke, modified and transformed by Berkeley, and exemplified in a still different form in Hume. This is not to suggest that Wordsworth thought philosophically, in any strict sense; but rather that he made the very assumption about perception that was the philosophical starting point for Locke, Berkeley and Hume. This assumption was that perception itself is essentially an inner experience. What we are immediately aware of when we perceive anything is an idea (or impression, or image) and out of the series of these ideas we somehow construct the concept of external objects in the world. The relation of ideas to that of which they are ideas is essentially problematic. Indeed, philosophy seemed largely confined within the boundaries of this problem for centuries, and only in the twentieth century, after the heroic struggles of Kant and Hegel, to find it relatively easy to escape.

When, instead of receiving immediate perceptual 'ideas', we reflect on what has happened in the past, we present ourselves once again with an 'idea'. And this idea is like, but is not identical with, the idea first received in perception. There is a kind of continuity, a qualitative similarity, between the idea received in perception and the idea of memory (see chapter two). The use of the very same word 'idea', or 'image', for the object of awareness in perception and in memory made the qualitative continuity easier to accept. Even Hume, who drew a distinction, speaking of 'impressions' in the case of sense-experience and of 'ideas' in the recollection of sense-experience, held, as we have seen, that impressions were distinguished from ideas only by their greater liveliness or vivacity. Sometimes the two could even be confused. It was against this philosophical background, then, that Wordsworth wrote. The stuff of perception and the stuff of memory was identical. The only difference between the different 'ideas' lay in their relation to the past, the present or the future, or in their actual quality of 'vivacity'.

There is no wonder, then, that in Wordsworth the 'image' (his word, on the whole, for the philosophers' 'ideas') has a curious ambiguity. It belongs sometimes to the external world, sometimes to the world of inner experience.

At different phases of his life it is probable that Wordsworth was attracted by a radically idealist solution to the problem of how these two worlds were related. Berkeley, after all, a full-blown idealist, had taken the bull by the horns and had argued that there were not two worlds, but only one. Nothing exists except ideas, and those spirits who have the ideas. It made no sense on his view to speak of a world of material substance, forever unperceived but causing in us ideas which are somehow copies of itself. Material things in any case could never be causes. Causation was an active bringing into being, or creation, possible only for spirits. Matter, if it did exist, would be 'inert'. But, so Berkeley argued, there is no need to invent such a concept as that of 'matter'. For since nothing can be a cause except a spirit, it is God, the supreme spirit, who causes us to have those ideas which we call the ideas of perception. The whole world of nature is a world of ideas; and we experience them because God causes us to do so, in a particular order, and in particular and regular sequences.

Wordsworth recalled how, in his childhood, he had been tempted by some such thoughts. 'I was often unable to think of external things as having external existence', he wrote, 'and I communed with all I saw as something not apart from but inherent in my own immaterial nature' (note to the Ode 'Intimations of Immortality' (notes dictated to Isabella Fenwick, 1843, known as the Fenwick Notes)). And he goes on to say, without much philosophical consistency, that he used to have to touch the wall as he went by on his way to school in order to recall himself from the 'abyss of idealism' (as if the 'ideas' received by the sense of touch were somehow different from other ideas, and gave an assurance of the existence of the material, external world; a proposition that Berkeley totally denied).

Later, in 1798, we know that Coleridge was attracted by similar theories; and this is a time when such was the friendship and mutual influence between Wordsworth and Coleridge that it is virtually impossible to separate the thoughts of one from the thoughts of the other. In that year Coleridge wrote the highly Idealist poem 'This Lime Tree Bower My Prison', in which he speaks of the world of nature, the perceived world, in the following lines:

> . . . so my friend
> Struck with joy's deepest calm, and gazing round
> On the wide view, may gaze till all doth seem
> Less gross than bodily, a living Thing
> That acts upon the mind, and with such hues
> As clothe the Almighty spirit, when he makes
> Spirits perceive his presence

The thought that God is the spirit whose ideas are shared with other spirits, or that in perceiving nature, we are in some sense perceiving God, clothed (or 'veiled' according to one version of the poem) but fully present, was central to Berkeley's philosophy. And in sending the lines to Southey, Coleridge explained them by stating that he was a Berkeleian. In the following year he christened his second son Berkeley. The influence on Wordsworth and the attraction for him can be inferred.

Thus, in order to understand the significance of memory for Wordsworth, it is essential to bear in mind what may be called the ontological ambiguity that he was inclined to ascribe to images or ideas in general. And the images of memory were especially ambiguous. For they were not only, like the ideas of perception, poised between the internal and the external: they carried also contrary emotional significance. Being caused by something that was past or lost, they carried an aura of sadness or regret. But being, nevertheless, in part real, they carried also the consolation of creation. 'Creation', in this context, is more properly 're-creation', of what would, without these images, have been lost.

Besides this philosophical background, Wordsworth was writing against a background of poetry and of aesthetic theory which he was largely to transform. In her book *Tradition and Experiment in Wordsworth's Lyrical Ballads* (Oxford, Oxford University Press, 1976) Mary Jacobus calls attention to the lyric tradition of the Nostalgia Poem, the sentimental Revisits, and to the agreeable melancholy of Bowles's sonnets, at one time greatly admired by both Wordsworth and Coleridge.

Out of these relatively simple genres arose a new introspection, introduced by Akenside (*Pleasures of the Imagination*, 1744). Akenside was primarily concerned not with recording a mere mood engendered by nature, but with the effect of nature, as external, on the inner world of the beholder. A new and altered edition of his poem appeared in 1772, and the alteration was such as to sharpen the concentration on mental phenomena. What the mind receives from nature is a reflection of nature itself in the form of an idea; but it is not a mere reflection. It is also something real and permanent, an impression, like an impression made on wax, an abiding entity.

> For not th'expanse
> Of living lakes in summer's noontide calm
> Reflects the bord'ring shade and sun-bright heav'ns
> With fairer semblance; not the sculptur'd gold
> More faithful keeps the graver's lively trace,
> Than he whose birth the sister powers of art
>   Propitious view'd, and from his genial star
> Shed influence to the seeds of fancy kind;
>   Than his attemper'd bosom must preserve
>   The seal of nature. There alone unchang'd
> Her form remains.

By 1790 Archibald Alison was writing, in *Essays on the Nature and Principles of Taste*, of the essential *activity* of mind in constructing aesthetic pleasures, whether these are derived from nature or from art. 'What is that Law of Mind', he asks, 'according to which in actual life the exercise of the imagination is excited, and what are the means by which in the different Fine Arts the artist is able to awaken this important exercise of the imagination and to exalt objects of simple and common pleasure into objects of Beauty or Sublimity?' His answer is that when we feel either beauty or sublimity in natural scenery, we do so because our minds create their own images, over and above those images immediately presented to eye or ear. And when this happens 'our hearts swell with emotion, of which the objects before us seem to afford no adequate cause' (*Essays* i.1.1). Alison takes it for granted, as we can see from this passage, that the 'images' we get from perception, and those we create ourselves and add to the perceptual experience, are not different in kind. It follows that the total of images we experience in the contemplation of nature or of art is not a collection of passive imprints or mirror-images of what is outside us. We contribute images of our own, and it is this that gives the emotional content to the whole experience.

In the second book of essays, Alison goes further. He argues that, since material objects themselves, by themselves, could not impress us with images possessing the properties of beauty or sublimity, with the emotional impact implied by these terms, we must regard such objects as beautiful or sublime only insofar as we take them to be *signs* of something other than themselves: 'The qualities of Matter are not to be considered as sublime or beautiful in themselves, but as being the signs or expressions of such qualities as, by the constitution of our nature, are fitted to produce pleasing or interesting emotions' (*Essays* ii.6.6). And there is even a hint that impressions received in childhood may have peculiar significance for us. 'While the objects of the material world are made to attract our infant eyes, there are latent ties by which they reach our hearts.' But they would not attract even our infant eyes unless they gave rise to extra, emotion-laden images to supplement, reinforce and render pleasurable the actual immediate images on the retina, received from the objects themselves. In Akenside, too, we can find the suggestion that it is not perception itself but the memory of perception and the images retained by memory that are saturated with meaning, and therefore fruitful for contemplation:

> but to man alone
> Of sublunary beings was it given
> Each fleeting impulse on the sensual powers
> At leisure to review; with equal eye
> To scan the passion of the stricken nerve
> Or the vague object striking; to conduct
> From sense, the portal turbulent and loud,
> Into the mind's wide palace one by one
> The frequent, pressing, fluctuating forms,
> And question and compare them.
> (*Pleasures of the Imagination*, II, 50)

We may be reminded of William James's view that it is only in memory that experience 'counts for us' (p. 61).

One of Wordsworth's earliest poems, 'An Evening Walk', is sometimes written off as an exercise in which Wordsworth was deliberately aiming to write a traditional 'landscape' poem. He himself to some extent confirms this by giving the reader exact topographical marks by which to orientate himself should he wish to take the same walk. Nevertheless it is possible to detect in the poem the beginnings of an interest, not merely in what the eye could see, but in what the mind could contribute to perception. And, in 1794, a year after the first publication of the poem, Wordsworth added, among other additions, these lines:

> Its sober charms can chase with sweet control
> Each idle thought and sanctify the soul
> And on the morbid passions pouring balm
> Resistless breathe a melancholy calm;
> Or through the mind, by magic influence
> Rapt into worlds beyond the reign of sense,
> Roll the bright train of never ending dreams
> That pass like rivers tinged with evening gleams . . .

The 'never ending dreams' are those extra images whose immediate stimulus was present sense-perception, but which came from memory, to enrich the present experience. Conventional, almost derivative, though these lines seem, they nevertheless foreshadow the mature Wordsworthian doctrine of the central role of memory in the creative act.

It is unnecessary to rehearse in detail the theory of poetry according to which, for Wordsworth, recollection was an essential element. In the Preface to the *Lyrical Ballads*, besides the definition of poetry as taking 'its origin from emotion recollected in tranquillity', there is also, in the 1802 version, a definition of the poet as one who 'has a disposition to be affected more than other men by absent things as if they were present; an ability of conjuring up in himself passions which are indeed far from being the same as those produced by real events, yet . . . do more nearly resemble the passions produced by real events, than anything which from the motions of their own minds merely, other men are accustomed to feel in themselves'.

For Wordsworth, then, the *absence* of a real object, in space or time, or both, was essential if it was to become an object of aesthetic power or pleasure. But to think of objects and events in their absence is to experience them again as image, not identical with the original experience, but like it, just as Hume's 'ideas' were both derived from 'impressions', and were so like impressions that sometimes the one could be mistaken for the other. Thus for Wordsworth, the image, though indubitably mental (as was, in a sense, the original perception), could sometimes be so clear and vivid that it approached to the condition of sensation. Thus he wrote:

> Unfading recollections! at this hour
> The heart is almost mine with which I felt,
> From some hill-top on sunny afternoons,
> The paper kite high among fleecy clouds
> Pull at her rein like an impetuous courser . . .
>   (*The Prelude*, book I, 491–5)

Through the image (though here, unusually, not a visual image) comes the feeling, *almost* in its original form.

It is not simply that the memory-image brings with it, and increases, the recollected emotion. If that were all, Wordsworth's poetry, both in theory and in practice, would have been little more than an extension of the nostalgic, or revisiting, poems of his predecessors. Even Hume had recognized that poetic genius and poetic or rhetorical imagination had an uncanny power of turning mere ideas into impressions actually felt, and that distance in space and time was prone to turn disagreeable into agreeable feelings (*Treatise of Human Nature*, Book II, Section 6). But there are also two other crucial points, both, it is true, hinted at by Alison, yet carried much further and developed by Wordsworth into the very heart and essence of poetry.

First, at the time of the original perception, some scenes carry with them a promise of images to come:

> Thus oft amid those fits of vulgar joy
> Which, through all seasons, on a child's pursuits
> Are prompt attendants, 'mid that giddy bliss
> Which like a tempest, works along the blood
> And is forgotten; even then I felt
> Gleams like the flashing of a shield; the earth
> And common face of Nature spake to me
> Rememberable things . . .
>   (*The Prelude*, I, 581–8)

And the same present announcement of future images is part of what is meant by the famous 'spots of Time' passage, later in *The Prelude*, where the crucial and significant moments which 'take their date from our first childhood' carry with them a 'renovating virtue'; and even at the time they are experienced seem heavy with significance:

> . . . I should need
> Colours and words that are unknown to man,
> To paint the visionary dreariness
> Which, while I looked all round for my lost guide,
> Invested moorland waste, and naked pool,
> The beacon crowning the lone eminence,
> The female and her garments vexed and tossed
> By the strong wind.
>
> (*The Prelude*, XII, 254–61)

The point lies in the word *visionary*.

The second point is more important. The significance of memory-images, the positive power they have over us, comes from the addition they make to present experiences. Immediately after the lines quoted above, Wordsworth writes of his return to the same scene, in the 'blessed hours of early love', the beloved at his side:

> And think ye not with radiance more sublime
> For these remembrances, and for the power
> They had left behind? So feeling comes in aid
> Of feeling, and diversity of strength
> Attends us, if but once we have been strong.
>
> (*The Prelude*, XII, 267–71)

We can, perhaps, usefully distinguish simple from complex among the pleasures and the meanings of memory. The simple satisfaction of recollection is expressed in the 1804 'Daffodils' ode:

> For oft, when on my couch I lie
> In vacant or in pensive mood,
> They flash upon that inward eye
> Which is the bliss of solitude;
> And then my heart with pleasure fills,
> And dances with the daffodils.
>
> (*Poems of the Imagination*)

This is no more than the excitement felt by W. H. Hudson at the actual power of visualizing, of framing images which bring back with them the original pleasures. The more complex function of memory, on the other hand, the active power which is capable of adding to and transforming the present perception, has its most explicit and elaborate expression in *Tintern Abbey*. Here, as Mary Jacobus has argued (op. cit., chapter 5), 'the poet's attitude to an unchanging landscape becomes a way of measuring the change that has taken place within'. The existence of his memory-images, retained during the five years between his visits, allows him to explore *his own continuous existence*, and to seek meaning in the emotions that are now, on a return to the same place, so powerfully experienced yet so changed. He is not passive but active: he brings to his present experience the images which were first impressed on his mind, then stored in memory and brought out for contemplation in the time between his visits. The description of the poet's return is an account not of physical or geographical phenomena, but of images, partly those images or impressions that are caused by present perception, partly those retained in his mind over the years. Nowhere in Wordsworth's writing is the ambiguity of the image, inner and outer, physiological and mental, more apparent or more important for the meaning of his poetry. Even the apparently straightforward description of the present scene at the beginning of the poem carries the sense that it is imbued with significance, because it is imbued with *thought*:

> Once again
> Do I behold these steep and lofty cliffs,
> That on a wild secluded scene impress
> Thoughts of more deep seclusion; and connect
> The landscape with the quiet of the sky

And then, quite explicitly, the regenerative power of memory-images themselves is explored:

> These beauteous forms,
> Through a long absence, have not been to me
> As is a landscape to a blind man's eye:
> But oft, in lonely rooms, and 'mid the din
> Of towns and cities, I have owed to them,
> In hours of weariness, sensations sweet,
> Felt in the blood and felt along the heart.

And at the end of the poem, when he turns to address Dorothy, seeing in her the same immediate openness to the impressions of nature that he had experienced five years before, he predicts that she too will retain images in memory that will rejuvenate her, and give point to her life.

> Oh! yet a little while
> May I behold in thee what I was once,
> My dear, dear Sister! and this prayer I make,
> Knowing that Nature never did betray
> The heart that loved her; 'tis her privilege,

Through all the years of this our life, to lead
From joy to joy: for she can so inform
The mind that is within us, so impress
With quietness and beauty, and so feed
With lofty thoughts, that neither evil tongues,
Rash judgments, nor the sneers of selfish men,
Nor greetings where no kindness is, nor all
The dreary intercourse of daily life,
Shall e'er prevail against us, or disturb
Our cheerful faith, that all which we behold
Is full of blessings. Therefore let the moon
Shine on thee in thy solitary walk;
And let the misty mountain-winds be free
To blow against thee: and, in after years,
When these wild ecstasies shall be matured
Into a sober pleasure; when thy mind
Shall be a mansion for all lovely forms,
Thy memory be as a dwelling-place
For all sweet sounds and harmonies; oh! then,
If solitude, or fear, or pain, or grief.
Should be thy portion, with what healing thoughts
Of tender joy wilt thou remember me,
And these my exhortations!

The capacity to retain memory-images, then, is a peculiar blessing.
The more powerful the first impressions made by nature on the
mind, especially the mind of a child, the firmer and stronger will be
the memory-images stored in the mind, and the more tolerable as
well as the more intelligible will the life of man become. It is for the
poet to explore the meaning of these images, and ensure that they
are permanent. In 1798 Wordsworth returned again and again to
this thought. For example, of the visionary Pedlar, he wrote:

While yet a child, and long before his time
He had perceived the presence and the power
Of greatness, and deep feelings had impressed
Great objects on his mind, with portraiture
And colour so distinct that on his mind
They lay like substances, and almost seemed
To haunt the bodily sense. He had received
A precious gift, for as he grew in years
With these impressions would he still compare
All his ideal stores, his shapes and forms,
And being still unsatisfied with aught

> Of dimmer character, he thence attained
> An *active* power to fasten images
> Upon his brain, and on their pictured lines
> Intensely brooded, even till they acquired
> The liveliness of dreams . . .
>
> (*The Pedlar*, 1798 version)

The Pedlar, as visionary or poet, was himself active in fastening and securing the impressions of nature, themselves so strong and firm that they were 'like substances'. But the true *value* of these images is discovered only when they become images of memory. The thought is yet more explicit in a fragment of the same year:

> . . . In many a walk
> At evening or by moonlight, or reclined
> At midday upon beds of forest moss
> Have we to Nature and her impulses
> Of our whole being made free gift, and when
> Our trance had left us, oft have we, by aid
> Of the impressions which it left behind,
> Looked inward on ourselves, and learned, perhaps,
> Something of what we are. Nor in those hours
> Did we destroy . . .
> The original impression of delight,
> But by such retrospect it was recalled
> To yet a second and a second life,
> While in this excitation of the mind
> A vivid pulse of sentiment and thought
> Beat palpably within us, and all shades
> Of consciousness were ours.

The images which, in *Tintern Abbey*, Wordsworth spoke of as restorative are themselves the vehicle, both of emotion, and of understanding. The 'forms of beauty' on which he was able to brood, in the absence of the scene itself, are such as to teach us, not only about ourselves, but about the nature of the universe. Our images when they have been stored in memory take on a significance which they could never have had as more immediate impressions on the senses. It was to the 'forms of beauty' that Wordsworth owed, he said, the gift of contemplation in which:

> . . . the affections lead us on,
> Until the breath of this corporeal frame,
> And even the motion of our human blood
> Almost suspended we are laid asleep
> In body and become a living soul:

> While with an eye made quiet by the power
> Of harmony and the deep power of joy,
> We see into the life of things . . .

As a poet he crucially *needs* the images of memory:

> Oh, mystery of man, from what a depth
> Proceed thy honours. I am lost, but see
> In simple childhood something of the base
> On which thy greatness stands . . .

> . . . The days gone by
> Return upon me almost from the dawn
> Of life: the hiding places of man's power
> Open; I would approach them, but they close.
> I see by glimpses now; when age comes on,
> May scarcely see at all; and I would give,
> While yet we may, as far as words can give,
> Substance and life to what I feel, enshrining,
> Such is my hope, the spirit of the Past
> For future restoration.
> (*The Prelude*, XII, 272–86)

There can never have been a greater demand made of the images of memory, nor a clearer statement of how these images, being loaded with significance themselves, are transformed into art, and thus into understanding. If the past is a paradise from which we have been excluded by the passage of time, we may nevertheless regain entry to it by the contemplation of the forms of nature, the images impressed upon us, and retained continuously since those past days.

However, by no means all the writers who have understood and exploited the relation of memory to art have held, as Wordsworth did, that it was through images that the power of memory was experienced. Just as some philosophers have thought of memory as a particular kind of knowledge, not dependent upon images of any kind, so there have been writers who have thought of art as deriving from and seeking to articulate this kind of knowledge, to which images may be irrelevant, even an impediment. The immediacy of the knowledge which constitutes memory is, on such a view, its peculiar mark. And so an image may seem to come between the artist and the knowledge which it is his concern to convey.

For an image may be thought of as a kind of picture (an inner picture, it is true, or an inner tape-recording), and if so, then it should be capable of being described. Accuracy in description would then be the artist's goal. As envisager, he should have little difficulty in conveying to his audience exactly what it is that he 'sees' or 'hears', albeit with his inner eyes and ears. Although it is true that I have my set of images, and you have yours, and so, in one sense, the images would be 'private', nevertheless, insofar as the image is a genuine reproduction of reality, words should be able to be found to make my image public, just as they can be found for a commonly intelligible account of the real world. To describe images is simply to borrow words designed to describe reality. Images may be thought of as kinds of photographs; and we know that we can describe photographs accurately enough, even to those who have not seen them. To think of images in this way is, of course, to strip them of their emotional content, and their peculiar and abiding significance, so apparent to Wordsworth. Treated as mere mechanical reproductions, they offer no salvation to one excluded from the paradise of the past.

On the other hand, the immediate knowledge of the past which may, alternatively, be thought to constitute memory is private in a different and more radical way. It is *essentially* emotional in character. Since it can be called knowledge, its object is what is true. But the truths are of the heart not of the head. They are truths which reveal what things are like, rather than simply what occurs or what is the case. About such knowledge there is an essential privacy. The significance of memory-knowledge may be enormous to the person who knows, who remembers, but he may fail to express this significance to anyone but himself. He may struggle, and fail, as someone may tell his dream, and fail completely, in the bare narrative, to convey its immense meaning. But, insofar as the narrator is an artist, it will be his over-riding aim to break through this barrier, and only if he can do so, and can communicate the truth that he knows, will he feel satisfaction. There are no ready-made words, like the words for colours or shapes, nor are there fixed classifications, like the classifications of birds and insects, to apply to the life of the emotions, yet the whole function of the artist is to communicate this life, directly or indirectly, and he has to discover the means to do it.

Artists, then, who are also theorists of art, have often tried to find words, not only for their knowledge, but for the creative power which makes a search for such knowledge and its expression possible, even imperative. Coleridge used the word 'joy' to designate the imaginative power essential to the poet, a power which arose out of the strength of his feelings when he contemplated that which he sought to describe. It was 'joy' that he tragically felt himself to have lost when, in 'Dejection: an Ode', he recorded that he 'saw, not felt, how beautiful things are'. Proust used the same word, 'la joie', as the mark of creative genius, and this joy was, in his view, essentially connected with the knowledge that comes from memory.

We must look next, then, at what is perhaps the most complete analysis of the connection between this 'joy' and the human memory. Towards the end of *À la recherche du temps perdu* (op. cit. pp. 95ff.), Proust describes how the narrator came out of a new sanatorium, no better, and full of depression. On the railway journey back to Paris he became convinced, for the hundredth time, that he had no literary talent. What made him so certain was the total absence of joy he experienced as he observed the effect of the light on the line of trees that ran along beside the railway. '"Trees", I thought, "you have nothing more to tell me; my cold heart hears you no more. I am in the midst of Nature, yet it is with boredom that my eyes observe the line which separates your luminous countenance from your shaded trunks. If ever I believed myself a poet, I now know that I am not one."' The following day, he decided to go to the Princess de Guermantes's reception (that reception at which he was to see everyone totally transformed by time). On the way he reflected on the absence of joy, and therefore, he thought, of talent, which had manifested itself to him the day before. Trying again, he began, as he says, 'to draw on my memory, for "snapshots", notably snapshots it had taken at Venice; but the mere mention of the word made Venice as boring to me as a photographic exhibition, and I was conscious of no more taste or talent, in visualizing what I had seen formerly, than yesterday in describing what I had observed with a meticulous and mournful eye'. But, suddenly and dramatically, everything changed. As he was approaching the Guermantes' mansion, in the courtyard, he stumbled, and, in recovering himself, stepped with one foot on a flagstone that was lower than the one beside it. At the feeling of the uneven stones under his feet, he was immediately flooded with an amazing delight, just as he had been before when he tasted the madeleine dipped in tea.

> The happiness which I now experienced was undoubtedly the same as that I felt when I ate the madeleine, the cause of which I had then postponed seeking. There was a purely material difference . . . A deep azure now intoxicated my eyes, a feeling of freshness, of dazzling light enveloped me, and, in my desire to capture the sensation, just as I had not dared to move when I tasted the madeleine, because of trying to conjure back what it reminded me of, I stood . . . repeating the movement of a moment ago, one foot

upon the higher flagstone, the other on the lower one. Merely repeating the movement was useless; but if . . . I succeeded in recapturing the *sensation which accompanied the movement*, again the intoxicating and elusive vision softly pervaded me as though it said 'grasp me as I float by you, if you can, and try to solve the enigma of the happiness I offer you'. And then, all at once, I recognized that Venice which my descriptive efforts and pretended snapshots of memory had failed to recall; the sensation I had once felt on two uneven slabs in the Baptistry of St Mark had been given back to me and was linked with all the other sensations of that and other days which had lingered, expectant in their place among the series of forgotten years from which a sudden change had imperiously called them forth.

The contrast here described between the failed attempt by the narrator to find creative joy through deliberately recalled 'snapshots' (no more fruitful than meticulously observed present perceptions) and the sudden surge of joy from the sensation of the uneven stones forms the basis for Proust's distinction between the voluntary and the involuntary memory. Voluntary memory is connected by him specifically with visual imagery. In the first volume of the novel (I, p. 57), he contrasts the efforts made in later life to recall the various different aspects of Combray with the immediate reliving of Combray which came to him, unannounced and unasked, through the taste of the madeleine (though even in this case, as in the case of the uneven paving stones, he had to think, to reflect on his sensation of joy, before he recognized the memory from which it, in fact, derived).

He could, at any time, he says, have informed people of various true facts about Combray. 'But since the facts which I should then have recalled would have been prompted only by an exercise of the will, by my intellectual memory, and since the pictures which that kind of memory shows us of the past, preserve nothing of the past itself, I should never have had any wish to ponder over this residue of Combray.' The intellectual is here implicitly identified with the visual; the voluntary or intellectual memory being that which can call up 'pictures'. In an interview with Elie-Joseph Bois for *Le Temps* (vol. 88, p. 289), Proust made the same point:

For me voluntary memory, which is, above all, memory of the intellect and of the eyes, gives us only the appearance, not the reality, of the past. But when a smell or a taste, rediscovered in totally different circumstances, reveals the past for us, in spite of ourselves, we feel how different this past is from what we thought we remembered, and what our voluntary memory painted for us, like bad painters who have their colours, but no truth.

Involuntary memory, then, gives us knowledge; indeed, if we pause to reflect on it, it constitutes direct knowledge of the past.

Is this the same distinction as was made, by Bergson (chapter 2, p. 28ff.), between spontaneous memory and the memory of habit? It is doubtful whether it is. Proust distinguished the voluntary from the involuntary; Bergson the habitual from the spontaneous. There are certainly points of similarity between the two, and the question of the influence of Bergson upon Proust has been a matter of considerable controversy. But questions of influence are of less importance than questions of interpretation. We may throw some light on the relevance of memory to art by considering both Bergson and Proust, but we shall be able to throw no greater light, if we could (as we cannot) establish the historical facts of influence.

There is, in any case, a danger of dichotomies. Once the delicious excitement has died down of distinguishing *a* from *b*, even more, of asserting that *a* is the *opposite* of *b*, the philosopher or critic is left with the presumption that everything in the world is either *a* or *b*. If two writers agree as to *a* it seems to follow inevitably that they must also agree as to *b*, since both are agreed that, logically, if a thing is not *a* it is *b*. So, since 'involuntary' appears to be the same as 'spontaneous' or, at least, to come fairly close to it, it has often been assumed that 'voluntary' must therefore be the same as 'habitual', the words used by Proust and by Bergson respectively. The meanings of the two words make this highly implausible.

Bergson, as we saw (chapter 2, p. 29), held that nothing is forgotten. At the level of the unconscious all experiences exist timelessly, since 'time' is a category imposed on experience by the habitual, conscious, workaday mind, turning the flow of experience into a manageable, spatially separate set of things, one succeeding another neatly. Habitual memory is that which we use every day to tell us what things are, and how we are to arrange them and use them. By habitual memory we learn to use language and to exercise skills. But, equally, habitual memory is reinforced by language, and the automatic classifications and distinctions inherent in it. To use habitual memory we need to be conscious and to think, and think linguistically.

In order to experience the timelessness of spontaneous memory, on the other hand, we need to fall into a trance-like state in which our sharp-eyed awareness of the external world, and our readiness to distinguish things that spatially differ in that world, is lulled to rest. The timeless activity of the human spirit, its free enterprises, can be experienced only in such a dreamlike condition. Though spontaneous memory gives knowledge, indeed, *is* a kind of knowledge, it is knowledge which cannot readily be passed on by one free spirit to another. It is entirely different from the scientific knowledge by which we live our practical lives and which we can teach to one another.

For Proust, on the other hand, involuntary memory is certainly not experienced at the level of the unconscious. For it essentially consists in the relating of a present felt experience to another similar experience in the past, which brings to the surface with it, when it is recalled, a whole train of related sensations and emotions. Involuntary memory brings sudden and intense significance to ordinary, even trivial, things in the outside world. Moreover, in order to bring to fruition the intense happiness which such a present experience may cause, a tremendous effort is needed, to capture exactly what it is that is being remembered. So although the beginning of the memory sequence is involuntary, and cannot be deliberately sought, it will hardly count as memory at all unless it is followed up, quite deliberately, and the associated feelings, the conjoined explicit recollections of the past, dragged up to the surface of the mind. The narrator had to concentrate his whole attention on the sensation of the uneven stones before he could recognize what it was that it recalled. If the effort of concentration is successful, then what is recalled is not merely the originally related sensation, but the whole emotional experience of that part of the past in which it occurred. The joy which this brings goes with the recognition that we now know, perfectly, how things were and are.

For because what we grasp is the past, and yet our knowledge and our deep happiness are part of the present, we have found a way to overcome the gap between past and present. We have achieved a universal and timeless understanding of what things are like. And with this comes the hope, though no more than this, that the truth of how things were/are can be shared. We may, with sufficient patience, be able to have the 'same thought' as those for whom we write. But having the same thought as another does not mean that we lose our own individuality. Far from it. My knowledge is mine, though I share it. My own continuous existence, as a separate individual, is what has made the knowledge possible, has, indeed, brought it into existence.

All this is possible through involuntary memory. Voluntary

memory, on the other hand, can give us nothing except superficial appearances. This is perhaps why Proust is so liable to equate the voluntary with the visual, and why, on the whole, he despises the visual image. For it is very natural to think of sight as telling us *merely* what things look like, as opposed to what they are.

It is certain, at any rate, that Proust thought of the superficial, the visual, and the verbal, as closely related, and 'mere words' on their own may be quite without power to cause feelings, just as mere images may. In the same way as the narrator could have listed the visual aspects of Combray without feeling any particular emotion, so Swann was able to talk perfectly neutrally about the time when he was loved by Odette, but was overcome by the emotional impact of the existing past, when he heard the 'little phrase' from the Vinteuil sonata. The music had a meaning for him that the words concealed.

And there is here perhaps a hint of 'habit memory' in one possible sense of the term. Proust is not much interested in the philosophical or psychological point that, in order to manage the world, to find our way about it, let alone to describe it, we have to be equipped with memory. But he fully understands that the more purely conventional a memory becomes, so that it can be 'called up' or repeated without thought, the less it is capable of bringing us to the truth to which, given luck, patience and effort on our part, involuntary memory may lead. A memory image, in particular a visual image, may get worn out with over-use, in the same way that a sight may become so familiar that it means nothing to us. It is not possible to summon at will the feelings, and therefore not the truth, of memory. This is why the memory that is central to art is called by Proust 'involuntary'. That which is irrelevant to art, the voluntary, may, in certain of its aspects, become habitual. A. E. Pilkington in his book *Bergson and his Influence* (Cambridge, Cambridge University Press, 1976) calls attention to the alienation from immediate reality which, for Proust, is brought about by habit. The alienation was referred to by Proust as 'analgesic'. It is illustrated by the passage in the novel in which the narrator writes to Gilberte. 'Her name, which previously he had been unable to write without immense emotion, he now puts down on the envelope with perfect detachment.' He 'puts no reality under the words'. The recollections of love, Proust wrote, are no exception to the general laws of memory, themselves subordinate to the yet more general laws of habit. Pilkington writes 'The power of something inherently trivial to resurrect the past, a power which important things or *familiar* sensations do not possess, springs from the fact that such a sensation is able to retain all its force, precisely because it does not "fade" through becoming habitual.'

It is perhaps because the vocabulary of smells and tastes, even of sounds, is so much less rich than that of sight that the purely visual is less likely to bring back the past in all its reality, and why Proust identifies the visual with the intellectual. Even a clear visual image can often be, like a word, a *mere* conventional sign. And the comparative richness of the vocabulary of sight is itself to be explained by the fact that, for most of us, unless we are blind, sight is the first of the senses by which we guide our practical life, find our way about and discriminate between one thing and another, as a preparation for action. A complete rediscovery of the past will doubtless include a recovery of its visual aspects. But the visual knowledge thus recovered will be different in kind from that which can be deliberately recalled.

Thus, when the narrator has tasted the madeleine dipped in tea, and when he is struggling to bring to the surface the memory which, because of the intense happiness he experiences, he knows is waiting to be discovered (which is, indeed, the significance of his taste of the tea), it is a visual image he searches for, and cannot at first call up.

> . . . feeling that my mind is growing fatigued without having any success to report, I compel it . . . to think of other things, to rest and refresh itself before the supreme attempt. And then, for the second time, I clear an empty space in front of it. I place in position before my mind's eye the still recent taste of that first mouthful and I feel something start within me, something that leaves its resting place and attempts to rise, something that has been embedded like an anchor at great depth; I do not know yet what it is, but I can feel it mounting slowly; I can measure the resistance, I can hear the echo of great spaces traversed. Undoubtedly what is thus palpitating in the depths of my being must be the image, the visual memory which, being linked to that taste, has tried to follow it into my conscious mind.

At last, after a final effort, the memory returns; and

> . . . immediately the old grey house upon the street where my aunt's room was rose up like the scenery of a theatre . . . and with the house, the town, from morning to night and in all weathers, the Square where I was sent before luncheon, the streets along which I used to run errands, the country roads we took if it was fine.

The visual recollection which has flooded in is far more than a 'snapshot'; far more than a single picture. It constitutes, in itself, complete knowledge of the past. And the narrator makes the point that the *sight* of the madeleine had done nothing to suggest the knowledge which, all the time, was hidden within him. Partly this was because he had so often seen such little cakes in bakers' shops in the interval, and so they had ceased to be peculiarly connected with Combray. But partly, he suggests, the visual simply is more liable to be buried or overlaid; while 'more faithful, the smell and taste of things remain poised a long time, like souls, ready to remind us, waiting and hoping for their moment; amid the ruin of all the rest; and bear unfaltering, in the tiny and almost impalpable drop of their essence, the vast structure of recollection' (I, p. 61).

If we are inclined to look here for influences on Proust (and in the case of so highly literary a writer, it is tempting to do so), the influence of Chateaubriand is probably more important than that of Bergson. Proust himself speaks of the *Mémoires d'Outre-Tombe*, both in a fragment of criticism called simply 'Chateaubriand', and also in the person of the narrator, at the end of the novel. 'Is not the most beautiful part of the *Mémoires d'Outre-Tombe*', he asks, 'of the same species as the tasting of the madeleine?' He goes on to suggest that such moments of memory combined with present sensation are more important than the great historical events which Chateaubriand recorded in his memoirs, since those events were events in time, whereas the moments of memory-knowledge were outside time.

Chateaubriand was quite explicitly interested in the central part played by memory in every aspect of life, as well as in the sudden moments of illumination that it can bring.

> What should we be without memory? We should forget our friendships, our loves, our pleasures, our work; the genius would be unable to collect his thoughts; the most ardent lover would lose his tenderness if he could remember nothing. Our existence would be reduced to the successive moments of a perpetually fading present; there would no longer be any past. Poor creatures that we are, our life is so vain that it is nothing but a reflection of our memory.
> (*Mémoires d'Outre-Tombe*, chapter 3)

He, like Proust, discovered the almost magical power of present sensations to call up memories. And the memories thus recalled seem, as Proust said, to exist outside time, and to give the person who remembers a hold on truth which is timeless; that is, to give him knowledge. Like Proust, he found that the present sensation which acted as the source of this knowledge was unlikely itself to be a visual experience. The best-known of the occasions he records was of hearing:

> I stopped to look at the sun; it was sinking into the clouds above the tower of Alluye from which Gabrielle d'Estrées, [the mistress of Henry IV], . . . had seen the sun set as I was seeing it now, 200 years before. I was distracted from these reflections by the warbling of a thrush, perched on the top-most branch of a birch tree. At that instant the . . . sound brought my father's domain before my eyes. I forgot the disasters I had recently witnessed, and carried suddenly into the past, I saw again that country where I had heard the thrush sing . . .

And with the vision of the country came also an intuition of the emotion he had felt when he used to hear the thrush in Combourg; the vague sadness which comes from a longing for happiness, which is yet mixed with the hope that happiness may be found, the vague sadness of inexperience. The other immediate sensation that Proust quotes from Chateaubriand was a smell, the heliotrope smell of a cluster of scarlet runners in flower: 'in that perfume, permeated by the light of dawn, of culture of life, there was all the melancholy of regret, of exile, of youth.'

Chateaubriand was aware both of the power and also of the essential privacy of memory. Writing about his childhood home of Combourg, he said, 'If, after reading this somewhat lengthy description, an artist took up his pencil, could he produce a good likeness of the château? I doubt it; and yet I can picture the château as clearly as if it were before my eyes.' (Indeed, in writing about it, he records that he had to stop. His heart was beating so hard as to push away the writing table at which he was at work. The memories wakening in his mind as he wrote were overwhelming in number and poignancy.) 'Such is the impotence of words and the power of memory to evoke material things. In beginning to speak of Combourg, I am singing the first couplets of a lament which will have charms for no one but myself'. (*Memories of Childhood and Youth*, MS of 1826)

We know, then, that Proust was moved, and perhaps influenced, by Chateaubriand. But in Proust the privacy of memory was not the end of the matter. For his joy in the apprehension of the real past was the joy of creativity: and in exploring its significance (an exploration postponed after the tasting of the madeleine), he discovered the relation between the real past and art. He discovered that he *must* turn the one into the other and that if he had time before his death, he *could* do so. One could argue, of course, that Chateaubriand too

believed this, and that the writing of his memoirs demonstrated that
he did. Proust, on the other hand, before acting on his belief,
formulated it as a theory. He recognized that memory was the key to
the lost paradise.

There are two crucial elements in the theory: the concept of time
and that of the self. These concepts together give rise to Proust's
belief in the truth of art, its unique power to reveal the essence of
things. After treading by accident on the uneven paving stones, the
narrator went in to the Guermantes' party; waiting in the library by
himself, before joining the Princesse de Guermantes' guests, he
experienced in close succession two more sense perceptions, each of
which, like the sensation of the uneven stones, transported him to
knowledge of the past. He heard the clink of a spoon against a cup (a
sound practically identical with that made by a maintenance man's
tapping of the wheels of a train); and he wiped his mouth on a
starched table-napkin, brought him by a considerate servant. Each of
the two occasions caused a separate and qualitatively different
moment of the past to be reborn, and lived again, just as the paving
stone episode had. Time, then, consists of a series of moments, most
of which are lost to us for ever; but they are somehow, nevertheless,
lying in wait, in case chance should bring us to a sensation connected
with them, or contained in them, which can drag them up out of
oblivion. For each past sensation is inextricably connected with
others. We do not experience impressions in isolation as, for
example, Hume and the British empiricists would have supposed.
Instead, all our senses are deployed at any particular temporal
moment. So if one sensation is revived, it drags with it the experience of the other senses, experiences which were at the original time
contemporary. 'An hour is not merely an hour, it is a vase filled with
perfumes, with projects, with climates' (XII, p. 238). To retrieve a
fragment of time is to retrieve something complete in itself like a
single complete chord played by an orchestra.

Similarly the personality, the series of experiences and attitudes
and emotions which go to make up one person, is not a coherent or
continuously conscious whole, but fragmentary. Yet the broken and
fragmentary self can be given a unity by the reliving of the past in the
present. Seeking to discover the cause of the amazing happiness he
felt in such moments as the tasting of the madeleine or the stepping
on the uneven stones, the narrator says 'In truth, the being within
me which sensed this impression, sensed what it had in common in
former days and now, sensed its extra-temporal character, a being
which appeared only when, through the medium of identity of

present with past, it found itself in the only setting in which it could exist and enjoy the essence of things, that is outside time.' The true self, that is, the self which is continuous throughout life, is revealed only at the moment of experiencing two fragments of time together, the present with the past.

Proust had no doubt that the imagination can work only upon what is not immediately present to it. And, therefore, insofar as the imagination is engaged with present experience, it must take the present as referring to something other than itself. Imagination is that which perceives the significance of experience, which reveals, that is to say, what experience means. Just as Coleridge records in his notebooks how he sought a meaning for certain powerful shapes which appeared before his eyes in the dark: 'O that I could but explain these concentric wrinkles in my spectra'; and as he frequently, by exact description of the visible scene, tried to give a sense beyond itself to what he meticulously depicted, so the narrator recalls that 'as far back as Combray I was attempting to concentrate my mind on a compelling image, a cloud, a triangle, a belfry, a flower, a pebble, believing that there was perhaps something else under those symbols which I ought to try to discover, a thought which these objects were expressing in the manner of hieroglyphic characters . . .' (XII, p. 225). And he recognized that the impulse behind his attempted readings of experience then, and his probing now into the nature of the happiness he felt in reliving the past, was the same impulse. It was the desire to know and to understand the nature of things. So what was given him by the experience of the madeleine or the uneven stones was not only a real moment of the past, but more than that, 'something which being common to the past and the present, is more essential than both . . .'

> . . . Let a sound, a scent already heard and breathed in the past be heard and breathed anew, simultaneously in the present and the past, real without being actual, ideal without being abstract, then instantly the permanent and characteristic essence hidden in things is freed and our true being which has for long seemed dead . . . awakes and revives . . . An instant liberated from the order of time has recreated in us man liberated from the same order so that he should be conscious of it. We understand that the name of death is meaningless to him, for, placed beyond time, how can he fear the future?

The authenticity of these rare moments of knowledge was manifest to the narrator. It would have been impossible to doubt whether or not they were illuminating. But yet the illumination had to be explored, and explored 'where it existed, that is within myself'. Such exploration could not be undertaken except by converting the immediate experience into something which could be communicated. Proust had to attempt to bring out his sensations from obscurity and convert them into their 'intellectual equivalent'. 'And what other means were open to me than in the creation of a work of art?' At the very end of the novel, we read 'the joy I experienced was not derived from a subjective nervous tension which isolates us from the past, but on the contrary from an extension of the consciousness in which the past, recreated and actualized, gave me, alas but for a moment, a sense of eternity. I wished that I could leave this behind me to enrich others with my treasure.' This is the voice of the artist, in the very process of turning memory into art. It is the voice of Wordsworth explaining that he *has* to pass on what he has seen and understood in the images of memory.

The difficulties for the artist are enormous. For Proust, the battle was a battle with language, and, particularly, a battle against the cliché. The narrator is shown to admire the painter, Elstir, especially for his genius in forgetting all learned and stock responses, forgetting even what things are called and what they are for, so that he can paint them as they really are. If God created, we are told, by conferring names on things, Elstir creates by taking them away. It was, I suppose, the painting of phenomenology. Husserl's philosophical method was described by him as 'putting the world in brackets'; and this meant putting out of mind all scientific knowledge, all preconceptions, everything learned, so that the essence of things as they were actually experienced could be revealed. This was what he meant by 'consulting the facts themselves'.

Such was the task Proust set himself, through the medium of words. The way to do it turned out to be the long attempt to present *himself*, a self whose continued real existence through time was now guaranteed by the truths revealed through memory, and whose uniqueness was to be shown through its own unique style of representation.

An artist who pursues this path will at least have the certainty that what is given to memory is true. It is precisely because real memory comes involuntarily and by chance, that we can be sure that it is true. There is nothing in it that is invented or factitious.

> I had not gone to see the two paving stones in the courtyard against which I had struck. But it was precisely the fortuitousness, the inevitability of the sensation which safeguarded the truth of the past it revived . . . since we feel its effort to rise upwards to the light and the *joy of the real recaptured*. That fortuitousness is the guardian of the truth

of the whole series of contemporary impressions which it brings in its train, with that infallible proportion of light and shade, of emphasis and omission, of memory and forgetfulness, of which the conscious memory or observation are ignorant.

Nothing that we deliberately think up has this inbuilt guarantee of truth.

That book which is the most arduous of all to decipher, is the only one which reality has dictated, the only one printed within us by reality itself. Whatever idea life has left in us, its material shape, mark of the impression it has made on us, is still the necessary pledge of its truth. The ideas formulated by the intellect have only a logical truth, a possible truth, their selection is arbitrary . . . It is not that the ideas we formulate may not be logically right, but that we do not know if they are true. Intuition alone is the criterion of truth and, for that reason, deserves to be accepted by the mind, because it alone is capable, if the mind can extract the truth, of bringing it to greater perfection, and of giving it pleasure without alloy.

The artist, then, does not invent, he merely tries to translate what he has come to know into a language which the world can understand: '. . . the duty and the task of the writer are those of an interpreter' (XII, p. 240). What he interprets are the truths revealed by memory, truths which are, of course, 'about' himself. But, because they are *certainly* true, they must be universally intelligible.

6

Self-exploration:
Diaries and Autobiographies

The poet or the novelist, with or without an aesthetic theory in his mind, may, as we have seen, seek to explore the path of truth through memory. But it is not the professional, the dedicated 'writer', alone who may feel impelled towards this exploration. The keeping of diaries and the writing of autobiographies are two further related forms of the passion for truth through memory. If we ask why people keep diaries, or write their autobiographies, the answer is not straightforward, but it is undoubtedly related to that sense of the continuity of the individual self which has emerged as something uniquely valuable to human beings. The value of being *myself*, a person who has survived through time, is a value shared by the most ordinary people as well as those exceptional and sometimes missionary figures who are professional writers .

We must first distinguish, in the case of both diaries and autobiographies, between the truly personal and exploratory and the impersonal or official. Richard Coe (*When the Grass was Taller: Autobiography and the Experience of Childhood*, London, Yale University Press, 1985) makes the distinction with regard to autobiography:

> In the great libraries of the world there are significantly fewer volumes of true autobiography than of memoirs. If the isolated self is to be transmuted into something durably significant, it needs to possess a vitality and originality which is very far from common; and it needs further to be spurred on by the imperious urge to impart a message or to impart a truth which may not be allowed to vanish, or else by a dose of vanity so strong that never, for one instant, can the author doubt that his own existence, in all its intimate and unmomentous detail, is supremely meaningful to the world at large.

Let us consider how this distinction applies to diaries. Those who write diaries specifically for publication, or more than half-thinking that their diaries will be published one day, have a difficult task. In the nature of the case, they have to write day by day, reflecting events as they occur, and referring to people as they cross the diarist's path. They are not allowed foresight (for they do not have it) but they must not too explicitly or regularly refer to the past. They write from, and of, the present. They record their dealings with the characters who make up the cast of their daily dramas, but they cannot do much to explain how the members of the cast came to be there or what their history is. They adopt the perspective of the present, within which their family, their friends and their colleagues are all familiar. For someone else to read a true diary, there is a need of footnotes. The reader has to be introduced to the characters as they crop up on the pages. Much that is familiar to the diarist, that is part of his daily life, will never be described. If he buys a new chair, he may describe it; but the chair he normally sits in will never be described. He may discuss his plans for a new lay-out for the garden, but not the appearance of the garden as it is now. However, those who write diaries for posterity are probably not much worried by this. They are more concerned with the great events of which they are a part, or the great people with whom they consort. Their diaries are, and are meant to be, a contribution to publicly accessible history; and when they are published, the necessary footnotes will undoubtedly be supplied. Such are the diaries of politicians. It is perhaps worth noticing that these can, like the diaries of Barbara Castle (*The Castle Diaries 1964–70, 1974–6*, London, Weidenfeld and Nicolson, 1980, 1984), be extraordinarily dull. Even the professional historian may wonder whether he needs to know quite as much about each individual Cabinet or committee meeting as he is told. By accident, on the other hand, they can be amusing or absorbing. The diaries of Richard Crossman (*The Diaries of a Cabinet Minister*, ed. Janet Morgan, London, Hamish Hamilton, 1975–7), equally political, nevertheless reveal a vain, self-important, vulnerable and entirely recognizable man, whom the reader feels in the end that he knows well, one aspect of whose life he has genuinely shared, like the life of a friend or colleague.

The contrast between the real and the 'memoir' diary is nowhere more strikingly illustrated than in the comparison between Evelyn's diary and that of Pepys. Pepys's diary, though of unique historical importance, becomes, as we read it, above all the diary of someone we know, and whose life we share. That we can so share the life of someone who lived in the seventeenth century of course adds greatly to the charm; but we read on, in the end, because of the diarist's character. Not so with Evelyn. This is a diary for historians, not for the common man.

It is difficult to guess whether or not Pepys, though he wrote in cypher, thought of his diary's being one day widely read. If not, the question is why did he write it? Why do any diarists keep diaries, if they do not think of them as adding to the sum of knowledge of a particular part of history, and therefore as essentially public? One answer to this question is that once they start, they get the habit. Pepys himself, when he thought his eyesight was failing, and so decided that he must give up his diary, recorded that it felt like a kind of death to abandon it. Frances Partridge (*Everything to Lose: Diaries 1945–1960*, London, Gollancz, 1985) writes, at the age of eighty, 'Diary-keeping is a difficult habit to break, and I must confess that I have failed to do so.' The writing of a diary ensures the real existence of the life we lead. If it is there on paper it happened, and was not a dream. If we write about what we did and thought, we can return to it; it is not gone for ever.

In this way a real diary is not so much an exploration or a celebration of memory as a substitute for it. Rather as a shopping list is a concrete object standing in the place of memory, or protecting us from forgetfulness, so a diary, it may be thought, should ideally be a record of everything that happened, everything that was thought or felt, as it was thought or felt, leaving no room for forgetfulness. A diary should render concrete and permanent that which would otherwise be fading and evanescent. It should be a shopping list in reverse. Viewed in this light, the diarist may think of his diary as something perhaps one day to be used. If he ever wanted to write his autobiography, or the story of some episode or other in his life, his diary would be there to be consulted. It would constitute the raw material out of which something else could be made, by himself or another.

In the introduction to his selection from Cecil Beaton's diaries (*Self-Portrait with Friends. The Selected Diaries of Cecil Beaton*, ed. Richard Buckle, London, Weidenfeld and Nicolson, 1979) Richard Buckle attempts to analyse the motives of the diarist, and the value of this particular diary: 'Among recorders of current events', he writes '. . . Beaton stands alone. Neither Sévigné nor Pepys, nor Walpole nor Greville, nor Nicolson nor Channon met . . . such a diversity of men and women, travelled in five continents during a world war, or spent a year in Hollywood designing the most successful film of all time.' True enough. Imagine Pepys in Hollywood. And apart from the obvious fact that these activities do not necessarily make Beaton's diaries more interesting than White's diary of Selborne, let alone more interesting than Pepys, such a list of events cannot constitute the whole reason for keeping a diary, rather than keeping records of a different sort. Indeed Cecil Beaton began to keep a diary when he was a schoolboy, when his motive cannot have been to record notable events, or meetings with the famous. Richard Buckle concedes this. For he says 'It is easy to understand why the diary was written. Started because Beaton had no close friend or relative to whom he could pour out his hopes, fears or dreams, it became, when life grew more exciting, a way of snatching at the fleeting moment.'

Buckle's first explanation of Beaton's schoolboy diary must be dismissed. It shows a misconception of the nature of diary-keeping to suppose that the existence of a 'close friend or relative' could be a substitute for it. Friends and relations might, it is true, by their proximity, prevent someone's keeping a diary, by ensuring that he had neither time nor privacy to do so. They might even cause someone to be so extroverted, so busy with joint activities or shared pleasures, that he had no inclination to reflect on what he was doing. Thus many children might never start a diary; other people might give it up on marriage. But a friend or sister or lover is no substitute for a diary. In childhood, for example, a brother or sister may be a constant companion, a much-loved ally, but still not a confidant. And later, however loving, trusted or resistant to boredom a friend may be, he cannot exactly fulfil the function of the diary's page. In the first place, though conversation with a friend often takes the form of narrative, the narrative itself needs to be written down if it is not to be lost, like the events themselves; or so the diarist feels. Secondly, if conversation takes the form, not of narrative, but of confession or the analysis of reactions, then this must be highly selective, and adapted to the sensibilities of the interlocutor. The diary, if it is narrative, has acquired a certain permanence. If it is confessional, it is supposed to be non-selective, honest and not tailored to fit any particular 'Other'. On these two counts, the diary and the conversation are not, and never could be, wholly interchangeable.

The diary cannot, however, be as simple, honest and true as we have made it sound. The question of selection naturally arises within the diary itself, and is complex. Richard Buckle's second suggested motive for Beaton, or any other diarist, needs further investigation. Beaton, he said, wanted, as his life became more exciting, to 'snatch at the fleeting moment'. This comes nearer the heart of the matter. But if that is what the diarist wants to do, it makes no difference to him whether his life 'becomes more exciting' or not. The desire to arrest the passage of time, to render permanent what would other-wise be lost, may be just as intense with regard to the trivial and easily forgotten as it is when things seem 'memorable', outstanding and exceptional. If the purpose of the diary is to catch and pin down the 'fleeting moment', then, since all moments are equally fleeting, all should be caught, whether funny or boring, ordinary or extraordinary, redounding to our credit or the reverse. But it does not need to be said that no diary could, in fact, record everything. And even if the diarist may think of his diary as a kind of recorder, it cannot simply reproduce 'what happened'. Imagine someone setting up a camera and a tape-recorder at the beginning of each day, and moving them around wherever he went, so that in the evening he could 'live the day again', playing over all the day's events. This, though arguably itself selective, would, in any case, be no substitute for a diary, even though to play over the recordings in later years might be fascinating, and might serve, like a diary, as an *aide-mémoire*.

The crucial difference between the diary and the other records lies in the fact that the diary is a *description*. And here we come upon a factor of great significance. A diary is, necessarily, written in language which can be good or bad for its recording purpose. Words follow after, perhaps *hours* after, the events they describe. They may be accurate or misleading, true or false, exact or approximate, literal or figurative. Even if someone were to write a sentence or two of his diary immediately he had finished whatever he was doing, still his diary would not be like those television cameras that follow shoppers around in book shops. It could not *simply* record. There is no such thing as a verbal record which mirrors or reflects what happened; though some accounts, of course, approach nearer to this than others.

The diarist not only chooses what to record at the end of each day, but chooses how, in what language, to record it. The selection is made according to different criteria if he is writing an honest and exploratory diary from those he would use if he was writing for publication, or jotting down materials for a comic short story, or engaging in conversation. In all of these more 'public' forms of description or narrative there is an element of the manipulative. If you ask whether I have had a good day at the office, I may reply with a selection of events such as I think will please you, or such as I believe you will be able to understand, without my having to enter into long explanations; I will choose my answer to suit you, or perhaps to instruct you, or seek your approval. The diarist, on the other hand, has no one to manipulate except himself. If the thought 'How will I seem?' or 'What sort of figure will I cut?' creeps in, then the diary has ceased to be 'pure'. There is no such thing as a 'pure' conversation. At its very best and most honest, in a conversation the thought of the other person's feelings, his interests, his liability to be hurt or even simply embarrassed, is a perfectly legitimate consideration. In a true diary, embarrassment has no place, except remembered embarrassment, half-purged by being recorded.

So, though there is inevitably selection in the writing of even the most private of diaries, the selection is of a different order from that employed when the diary is to be published, or when it is thought of as designed perhaps for one other, an extended conversation or letter. For example, in a diary we need not trouble about appearing self-obsessed, never a way we would like our friends to describe us. We *are* self-obsessed, in the very act of writing the diary. Our triumphs and failures can be properly and accurately noted. We can even record, if we wish, who laughed at our jokes. Like Mr Pooter, we can record that 'Carrie roared'. Perhaps Mr Pooter is not far below the surface of any diary-writer.

Though the later publisher of a diary, if there is one, will have to select from the diary itself, the diarist will properly include much that might, to the general public, seem boring and trivial. For the diarist is trying to be truthful, and to encapsulate in words the flavour of his days, which may by no means be conveyed by leaving out the trivial or the tedious. He writes always against a background of the ideal of completeness and truth. He will, in fact, have little use for the concept of the 'boring', since the truth, when it is achieved, will not bore him, and may even not bore others, if others there are. If we, the reading public, read diaries which are too obviously selections, we may feel cheated of the truth, just as keen lovers of cricket feel cheated by being offered 'highlights' of the Test Match coverage. For if, in reading a published diary, we come to know the author as a friend, the question of boredom does not arise. To a friend, all friends are interesting.

Let us return to the concept of 'the fleeting moment'. The point of snatching at it is to pin it down, preserve it, and thus to be able, on demand, to re-animate it. The desire to pin it down in words is the same as the desire to be truthful; and being truthful, in a diary, demands that the diarist write every day (or whenever he can) about *that* day, the day that has just finished. He may prefer to omit days when he has had no time to write, rather than 'make them up'. For if he begins to summarize, or write the story of a week or a month instead of a day, he becomes immediately aware of his own intervention as a retrospective interpreter. Today it began to rain, and I was delighted because of the lettuces I had just thinned and planted out. I did not then know that it was the beginning of a week of deluging rain, in which the river was to flood, the seedlings be washed away, and during which I was to begin to suffer the acute melancholy of a wasted summer. If I wrote my diary as I ought, each successive stage, both of the weather and of my state of mind, would have been unfolded without foresight. If, on the other hand, I sum up at the end of the week, the reality of the gradual unfolding is lost. The denouement precedes the prologue. There is neither truth nor drama. The peculiar truth of a diary demands that each day be written as it comes.

But the truth is not easy to attain. The diarist, as we have seen, has to *try* for the truth. He has to decide what was important, what it was really like, how he really reacted, and then he has to seek words to describe it. If he is thus *seeking* truth, he cannot always or necessarily find it. There is no magic way of saying how things were, even as short a time ago as yesterday, or this morning. The diarist may not be very good at finding the right language; or he may deceive himself about how it really was. This is something which in its own right deserves investigation (see Anthony Palmer, *Proceedings of the Aristotelian Society*, supplementary volume, Self-Deception, 1972).

According to Sartre (*Being and Nothingness*, part I) the being-for-himself, or conscious being, is not only to some extent self-conscious all the time, aware that it is 'he' having the experiences that he has, as he has them, but he is also essentially capable of self-deception. He may describe himself (to himself or others) in ways that he knows, in one sense, are misdescriptions, or do not contain the whole truth. Human thought entails the ability to think of things not only as they are but also as they are not. This, though Sartre does not explicitly say so, is a function of the verbal or linguistic nature of human thought. If I can describe something rightly, my words must also be capable of describing something else wrongly. If I truly say that a road is straight, it follows that I could say this falsely of a crooked road, or falsely say of this road that it is not straight. The falsehoods would make sense; and only so can the truths make sense. It follows that, with regard to myself, I must be able to grasp not only what I am but what I am not, and to stand back and see myself in a detached way as this or as that. And so, according to Sartre, I must be able to play a part, or adopt a role, to pretend to be something that I can imagine myself being. If I can, on some occasions, see myself, and describe myself, as a mother, then I must also be able to decide that such is my role, and, temporarily or permanently, play it for all it is worth. Self-deception consists in pretending to be something. This does not necessarily mean that, in order to be deceiving myself, I must pretend to be something that I am not; it is more a matter of pretending to be *only* or *nothing but* that in terms of which I, for the time being, have chosen to describe myself. To over-play one's part is, in Sartre's terminology, to act in Bad Faith. A man may in truth be the father of children; yet he may deceive himself insofar as he pretends, from time to time, that he is completely absorbed in 'being a father', when he takes his children to the zoo, or enters, with slightly too much conscious enthusiasm, into their games. If this same man is a diarist, it is possible, even likely, that he will write his diary in Bad Faith. Just as he went to the zoo, acting the part of the loving and devoted father, in partial Bad Faith, so he will record his visit when he settles to write his diary in the evening. We may, after all, live our lives and write our diaries, intimate and private though they are, according to the self-same clichés.

If I believe that I have to love my parents, that this is what everyone does, and what is not only right but inevitable, then I may believe that love is what I feel; and if affectionate words and gestures are demanded, I will produce them. It is a very sophisticated child who can pick his way through such expected reactions. If I am a diarist, the conventional words may well be reproduced in my diary: grief when my mother goes away for a week, delight when she returns. For a young child it is almost impossible to distinguish the conventional and expected from the real: the cliché description from the 'true' description. Children believe that they ought to enjoy themselves when they go out to tea, and will say that they have, in the teeth of the evidence. A newly-displaced child, confronted day after day by the outrage of her new brother, may repeat the words 'Tom is a *nice* baby', and she may partly, but only partly, believe it. Her words are little indication of how she feels; but she has no better words to describe how she feels. If, impossibly, she were a diary-keeper, the banalities she utters, 'Tom is a nice baby', might well be entered in the diary. Only gradually, and painfully, might the diary become the recipient of the expression of more dubious emotions.

Gradually an awareness of the possibilities not only of deception but of self-deception may grow. It is likely that the keeping of a diary may be part of such growth, or may considerably hasten it. Sartre in his bleak autobiography (*Words*, translated by Irene Clephane, London, Penguin Books, 1967) looking back on his childhood sees himself as perpetually playing a part, but he cannot decide, looking back, at what time he realized his own insincerity (p. 45): 'I realized afterwards that it is possible to know everything about our affections except their strength; that is to say, their sincerity. Actions themselves will not serve as a standard unless it has been proved that they are not gestures, which is not always easy.' His own play-acting was all undertaken for the sake of the grown-ups through whose eyes he, an only child, had learned to see himself. Speaking of a time when he had begun to suspect his own sincerity, he writes 'I went into the kitchen, announcing that I wanted to shake the salad. There would be cries and shrieks of laughter: "No, darling, not like that. Hold your little hand tight. That's it. Marie, help him. See how well he's doing it." I was a bogus child holding a bogus salad-basket; I could feel my actions changing into gestures.' If Sartre had kept a diary then, which, of course, he was too young to do, he would probably have reported the gestures as acts. But, doing so, he might have begun to see them as they were, acts becoming gestures under the eye of the doting grown-ups, the recognition of showing-off, for that it was. For the motive of the diary-writer is largely to explore; to find out how things are by saying as exactly as possible what they were like, from one point of view, and from the vantage-point of one central agent.

The truth, if it can be discovered, can also, necessarily, be shared. But this is a misleading way to put it. The struggle to discover it and the struggle to share it are one and the same. This is as much so in the case of a diary never intended to be read by any eye other than the diarist's as it is in the case of a novel or any other work, destined from the outset for publication. Merely to state what is true is potentially to communicate it; for language, even a code or a cypher, is essentially, not just accidentally, common.

If I read a diary successfully written by someone else, the truth I learn from it, the knowledge that is shared in it, is knowledge of another person. It is like the knowledge I get when I fall in love with someone or make a new friend. An individual person is revealed. The diarist himself, re-reading his diary after a lapse of time, will also regain knowledge of his own past, not just a knowledge that this or that occurred, but, often, a reliving, the peculiar knowledge that is memory. Unless he refers to his diary merely for information, to find out what he gave the Smiths when they last came to dinner, or which day last year he planted the French beans, he will read it in search of a revelation or intuition of the past that is *his* past.

To be able to recreate his past through the language he then used is thus part of the diarist's motive. But the insight he gains through his diary is not intended to be wholly confined to him. The *common*, shared, nature of language ensures this. Charles Taylor, in his essay 'Language and Human Nature' (in *Human Agency and Language*, Cambridge, CUP, 1985), suggests that on an expressive view of language (a view which since the Romantic era we have hardly been able to avoid), in attempting to find words for our experiences, we are actually creating ourselves and our world. 'Of course our developing language, insofar as it is descriptive language, responds to the shape of things around us. But . . . there is another dimension to language, that by which its development shapes our emotions and relations. Expression shapes our human lives . . . What is made manifest is not exclusively, not even mainly, a self but a world.' The diarist is essentially concerned with recording his day in the best, most accurate and expressive language. Taylor says:

> Language is not merely the external clothing of thought, nor a simple instrument which ought, in principle, to be fully in our control. It is more like a medium in which we are plunged, and which we cannot fully plumb . . . It is not just the medium in virtue of which we can describe the world, but also that in virtue of which we are capable of the human emotions and of standing in specifically human relations to each other. (p. 235)

An emotion cannot be described and catalogued without an attempt to describe the situation in which the emotion arose. It is not like a pain which, though in one sense doubtless indescribable, can at least generally be identified by simple location. 'Tonight my thumb hurt'; 'I woke up with a headache.' On the contrary, such complex and essentially human emotions as shame, guilt, embarrassment, jealousy or love must be identified by way of a description of their objects, that towards which they are directed. The diarist may describe an occasion, and his feelings of disquiet at his involvement in it. It may be only as he writes (or, later, as he reads what he has written) that he can identify his emotion by name. 'I was jealous', 'I was frightened', 'I was ashamed.' Understanding the object, through the medium of such descriptions, seems actually to constitute, in some part, the particular nature of the emotion itself. It cannot be grasped except through the description of its object. To realize himself as an individual human being, capable of such human emotions (and to be potentially at least recognized as such by another human being who could understand the words if he read them), must lie at the heart of the diarist's project. Virginia Woolf, writing about her own exploration of her past, wrote 'The past is beautiful because one never realizes an emotion at the time. It expands later; and thus we don't have complete emotions about the present, only about the past' (*Moments of Being*, unpublished autobiographical writings, ed. J. Schulkind, London, 1985, p. 80). It seems to me that this 'expansion' is accomplished through language.

Though there is a peculiar insight into himself and his world that a diarist may achieve, he may nevertheless learn little about his own *character*, or his propensities or tendencies, from the keeping of his diary. Sartre speaks of the 'original project' of each human being, the way in which he chooses to experience his life, to react to his own circumstance and limitations. An outsider, another reader than himself, is much more likely than the diarist himself to say 'He is a snob' or 'He resents his brother's success.' The outsider, being separate and different from him, may have little hesitation in characterizing him as this or that. The diarist, recalling the events and the feelings and thoughts as they are recorded in his diary, recalls them moment by moment from the inside. Even if such words as 'jealousy' or 'resentment' may fit his feelings on one day, he will not necessarily believe that the description 'jealous' or 'resentful' fits him essentially or in the long term. I may read in my diary of twenty different occasions on which I was late for an appointment without its ever seeming appropriate to describe myself as unpunctual.

But re-reading a diary may sometimes lead a diarist to make the attempt not only to relive and recall the exact quality of the days he spent, the anxieties he had, the sensations or emotions that namelessly accompanied the recorded events, but also to objectify himself and his life. At this stage he turns upon his own consciousness to analyse and characterize it. He become like a biographer who might use a diary as evidence, rather than as a source of direct or immediate knowledge. He is ready to become his own biographer.

The art of biography is, in essence, no different from that of autobiography. Both are 'historical', even if not 'official'. (An autobiography need not fall into the category of 'memoirs' to be a contribution to history.) On the other hand, the difference between autobiography and diary-writing lies in their relation to time. If someone embarks on autobiographical writing, he is surveying his life, or the part of it so far lived, from a particular point in time, as a story, with a beginning and a middle, if not yet an end.

Sometimes autobiographers include within their books extracts from their own diaries. The difference of style and of viewpoint is immediate. In Simone de Beauvoir's volumes of autobiography (*Memoirs of a Dutiful Daughter*, translated by J. Kirkup, London, Penguin, 1959; *The Prime of Life*, translated by P. Green, London, Penguin, 1962; *Force of Circumstance*, translated by R. Howard, London, Penguin, 1965) for example, the contrast is striking. She did not always keep a diary, but when she did, it was of a 'true' and revealing kind. The author of the autobiography is a moralizer, a philosopher, a drawer of conclusions. As a diarist she is different. She sets out in her new car, and exclaims over the immense sense of freedom and power that goes with driving off by herself. She makes resolutions ('tomorrow I *will* start work'); she suffers anxiety and self-doubt. It is only as a diarist that she could conceivably be a friend. As an autobiographer, she is deliberately historical, aiming to put on record her relations with Sartre, and the nature of the political and literary world in which they lived.

Sartre himself held that there was little significant difference between biography and autobiography. Both were essential to history, and indeed were the proper material out of which history must be made. Towards the end of his life, he developed a theory of history which elaborated this thought. Accepting a broadly Marxist theory of history, that it consists of a dialectical clash between different economic classes, he nevertheless held that an account of such a class conflict cannot intelligibly be wholly materialist. It needs to be 'interiorized' before it can be understood. The writer, on his view, has a duty to present the dialectical process of history from the standpoint of individual people who, formed within a particular socio-economic context, live their own lives with particular and individual interests and insights. The projects they personally form become part of the thrust forward into the future of their contemporaries collectively. Just as the concept of the past is derived from 'my past', so that of the future is made up of 'my projects' and 'your projects'. To present this truth intelligibly is the work of the biographer *or* the autobiographer. If everything could be told about a man, whether by himself or another, then everything would be understood about history. In an interview with Michel Contat and Michel Rybalka, Sartre, speaking of his own biography of Flaubert, said:

> The most important project in the *Flaubert* is to show that fundamentally everything can be communicated; that, without being God, but simply as a man like any other, one can manage to understand another man perfectly, if one has access to all the necessary elements. I can deal with Flaubert; I know him, and that is my goal, to prove that everyone is perfectly knowable, as long as one uses the appropriate method. (*Situations*, X, Paris, 1976, p. 94)

Both biographer and autobiographer, then, are concerned, according to Sartre's theory, to reveal how a particular individual was formed by his circumstances, and how he, in turn, formed the future, by his particular acts and interests. Whoever tells the story, the aim must be to show what it was like to live and work within certain precisely described social assumptions and familial pressures, pressures peculiar to the individual and making him what he was. Whether Sartre wrote about Flaubert, or Baudelaire, or about himself, he wanted to expose the forces which made a man write, and what the justification for his writing was, in terms of history as a whole. In such an exposition, the account of childhood is of unique importance (*The Problem of Method*, translated by Hazel Barnes, London, Methuen, 1964, p. 62) 'The family is experienced as an absolute in the depth and opaqueness of childhood' and 'It is childhood which sets us insurpassable prejudices and . . . makes us experience the fact of belonging to a specific environment as a unique event.' Childhood experiences, that is to say, are not to be understood, as Freud might seem to understand them, as *causing* us to be as we are. It is rather that we cannot understand or explain what we are without reference to our childhood.

Even if we are not committed to a Marxist theory of the dialectic of history, we may, I believe, accept Sartre's view. His account at least presents one important aspect of biography and autobiography, the point of which must be to uncover as far as possible the presumptions and presuppositions within which a subject lived. Such presuppositions may be revealed in 'reliving' the life of the subject, as it seemed to him at the time. This is the philosophical justification for the writing of 'lives'. We are enabled to understand what it was like to be that person, living at that time, and growing up within such a family. We may be reminded of R. G. Collingwood, who held that it was the function of history to be 'self-revelatory' (*The Idea of History*, ed. T. M. Knox, Oxford, Oxford University Press, 1946, p. 18): 'History exists to tell man what he is by telling him what he has done.' The transition from the particular man to man in general is made when we can 'think the thoughts' of the subject of the history. For then the reader can identify himself with the subject, and feel that what the subject experienced he, the reader, is experiencing as well. Just as a novel, if it grasps the truth, may enable us to think the thoughts of the author, and show them to be universal, because shared, so history, on Collingwood's view of it, presents universal truths. We do not, when we think the thoughts of a person in the past, cease to be ourselves, nor cease to live in the present. It is rather that our thinking his thoughts, and understanding how it was to be him, transcends the barrier of time.

An example of an autobiographical passage where the author quite deliberately stands back from himself in his childhood, and attempts to uncover the presuppositions within which he lived, is to be found in an entirely 'pure', non-memoir autobiography (for it has to be said that 'memoirs' are, as Richard Coe said, more numerous than 'true' autobiographies; and that there are even more authors of memoirs who are motivated by vanity or the false notion that an 'interesting' life makes an interesting book, than there are diarists with this kind of motivation). This is the autobiography of L. E. Jones (*A Victorian Boyhood*, London, Macmillan, 1955):

> Before I leave childhood for boyhood, I am inclined to pause and take stock of the state of this young Norfolk family in the middle of the nineties. What did we know about the world we lived in? What were our pains and pleasures, our affections and emotions? That this was a world of preordained classes we never doubted. We felt no sense of patronage when, on Christmas Eve, the cottagers on the estate crowded into the decorated Servants' Hall, each man bringing with him a capacious red-and-white spotted handkerchief. This he unrolled upon a long trestle table and we children set upon each handkerchief . . . a chunk of raw and bleeding beef, and a packet of raisins done up in thick purple paper with a piece of holly stuck into it . . . We were not class-conscious because class was something that was there, like the rest of the phenomenal world.

And he goes on in this same analytic passage to discuss the actual economic circumstances of the tenants and their political views and those of his parents. The contrast between the facts, and what was known and understood of the facts by a child, is the point and the successful justification of the writing.

A comparable passage, this time describing the dawning awareness not of gross class difference but of class nuances, is to be found in Henry Green's autobiography *Pack My Bag* (London, Hogarth Press, 1940). He is describing the time in the First World War, himself as a young child, when his parents' house was used as an officers' hospital:

> I began to learn the half-tones of class, or, if not to learn because I was too young, to see enough to recognize the echoes later when I came to hear them. Manners I now know were what they had not got . . . Manners may be a way of making, say, kings and peasants easy together under a roof, they may come from a confidence in himself which is the usual attribute of a moneyed person. We had those manners and I believe my parents made everyone easy at our hospital, but what was interesting was the effect on them and on myself. One of the first took out my father's gun, his cartridges and

his dog and shot his pheasants out of season without asking. I remember that what upset us as much was the behaviour of my father's dog, that it should lend itself to such practices.

He then explains how, in the end, rules of behaviour had to be introduced by the officers in charge, and how this began to be like what he later encountered at school, not 'manners', but 'behaviour' enforced through the fear of penalty.

Such passages as these, then, could be biographical or auto-biographical. Their intention (at least in the two cases quoted) is sociological, to explain what it meant to live in a particular class-dominated society. The two passages are curiously similar, though the time described separated by more than a decade. The similarities could themselves be objectively analysed: they are both from the autobiographies of privileged male English persons, both Etonians, both writers, though of very different sorts, as it turned out. Obviously there is the possibility in such 'sociological' writing of getting things wrong. But, on the whole, such writing is designed to probe those areas where deception, and especially self-deception, might be lurking.

To return to L. E. Jones: speaking of his moral upbringing, he explains how his mother demanded from her children displays of affection and pleasure, as part of proper behaviour, thus introducing her children to a kind of hypocrisy which the grown-up Jones deplores (partly because it led him for a time to the opposite extreme, of what he calls 'unpalatable candour'). 'A rule in the discipline of white hypocrisy', he wrote, 'was that, whatever our ploys or games out of doors . . . at the first appearance of a parent, we must down tools, or swords or spears, and run, with love and eagerness in our faces, and greet him or her. Run we must, pumping up eagerness from nowhere as best we could, and enchanting my mother, I have no doubt, by this evidence of our ever-loving hearts.' How much did the child understand at the time what was going on in him? He realized, no doubt, his own reluctance, and the irritation of being interrupted in his game in which, Jones says, he was 'seeking asylum'. It was only later, however, that it could be recognized as hypocrisy or deception. We are reminded of Sartre: 'I realized afterwards that it is possible to know everything about our affections except their strength; that is to say, their sincerity.'

To uncover such habits of thought, demanded or spontaneous, conscious or below the level of consciousness, is the purpose of this kind of history. To begin to understand them is like beginning to understand, say, the demands and myths of chivalry, or the obligations and half-beliefs of Roman religion. Such is the point of history, but here mediated through somebody's memory of how things were. The more vivid the memory, and the more shrewd the author's analysis of the setting, the more the reader will feel that he understands, and has come upon a perfectly general truth. Regarded in this light, then, history, biography and autobiography are all one enterprise, an attempt to 'relive' the past, and so to understand man in his context, temporal and geographical.

Looked at in another way, however, the gap between biography and autobiography, still more the gap between autobiography and regular history, is immense. The search for truth can be regarded as different in kind; not the elaboration or analysis of myths, but the confrontation of immediate experience for its own sake. According to this account, the truth to be uncovered is not in any sense sociological, but personal, and nothing but personal. If the autobiography, conceived thus, succeeds in passing on knowledge, it is knowledge of that direct kind that constitutes memory itself. Memory-knowledge, as we have seen, is central to the concept of a person, and so it is the nature of a person that is revealed in autobiography. The justification for writing autobiography, even on this view, must of course be that any truth, once discovered, can be shared. And for some people, driven to self-exploration and self-discovery, the sharing of truth feels like an obligation. At the very least, it is a powerful desire. What is revealed in memory is a personal possession; but one that makes demands on its possessor. It demands to be shared. In his autobiography of childhood, *The Watcher on the Cast-Iron Balcony* (London, Faber and Faber, 1963), Hal Porter writes thus of his childhood house in Australia: 'Of this house, of what takes place within it until I am six, I alone can tell. That is, perhaps, why I must tell. No one but I will know if a lie be told, therefore I must try for the truth which is the blood and breath and nerves of the elaborate and unimportant facts.'

On this view, then, the truth in autobiographical writing is immediately revealed to the author. His task, as we have seen, is to try to find language to express it. Though tomorrow he may think that the truth discovered today was only partial, he cannot believe that he was totally deceived, if the knowledge came to him through memory. To avoid deception it is necessary only to concentrate on the memory itself, as Proust had to concentrate, and make an effort, to extract the truth from his feelings once memory was activated. Rousseau (*Confessions*, book 7) expresses this view of autobiography, probably for the first time (see also Anthony Palmer, op. cit.): 'I have only one faithful guide upon which I can rely, that is the chain of feelings which have marked the development of my being, and by means of them, that of the events that were their causes and effects. I may make factual omissions, transpositions, mistakes about dates, but I cannot go wrong about what I have felt, nor about what my feelings have led me to do, and that is what it is all about.' At the end of the *Confessions*, he says, 'I have told the truth. If anyone knows anything contrary to what I have here recorded, though he prove it a thousand times, his knowledge is a lie and an imposture.' Rousseau believed, then, that he had been able to re-create the 'chain of feelings' with absolute certainty; and to do this was to create for his readers *himself*, the person he was when he wrote, necessarily connected by the 'chain' to the person he had been in his past.

We may feel entitled to ask, What is the point of this re-creation? Why not allow this past person to die? His reanimation is a struggle; so what makes it worth while? There are plenty of human beings alive and all around us. Why is it necessary to try to preserve one, in the pages of a book? The same questions, as we saw, might arise in the case of diary-keeping. If part of the aim of the diarist is to snatch at the fleeting moment, we may raise the question, What is so good about *that* moment, the moment he tries to pin down? There are infinitely many other moments on the way. There is more sense, we might argue, in enjoying the next moment than in trying desperately to revive those that are past. Nostalgia is, after all, generally agreed to be a debilitating disease.

The answer is that the autobiographer, and the diarist too, insofar as his diary may reveal himself, feels himself, presented in his writing, to be in possession of a truth that no one else yet understands. This in itself is his motive for recording and communicating it. The first paragraphs of Henry Green's autobiography, from which I have already quoted, state this motive unambiguously:

I was born a mouth-breather with a silver spoon in 1905, three years after one war and nine before another, too late for both. But not too late for the war which seems to be coming upon us now . . . That is my excuse that we who may not have time to write anything else must do what we now can. If we have no time to chew another book over, we must turn to what first comes to mind, and that must be how one changed from boy to man, how one lived, things and people and one's attitude. All of these otherwise would be used in novels, material is better in that form, or any other that is not directly personal, but we feel we no longer have the time. We should be taking stock.

Taking stock is the sorting through of possessions before they can get lost or confused, to see what there is. The material, that is to say the truths, could have been used for the material of imaginative literature, Green says. But the use to which they are put is itself a work of imagination, in the sense that any search after expression in language is so. Language, as we have suggested, creates as it records. It is worth referring again to Sartre. He has no doubt about the imaginative character of biographical or autobiographical writing. He says, in the interview from which I quoted earlier (p. 114), and speaking of his *Flaubert*, 'I would like it to be read with the idea in mind that it is true, a true novel. Throughout the book, Flaubert is presented the way I imagine him to have been, but since I used what I think were rigorous methods, this should also be Flaubert as he really is, as he really was. At every moment in this study, I use my imagination.' The concept of the 'true novel' is, of course, one that exactly fits Proust's novel. It is a description designed to bring out the *universality* of truth, however that is related to individual circumstances or particular lives.

There is no doubt that what Henry Green had and felt he must not lose or waste was *memory-knowledge* of what things were like. Soon after the passage quoted he says:

> If I say I remember, as it seems to me I do, one of the maids, that poor thing whose breath smelled, come in one morning to tell us that the *Titanic* had gone down, it may be that much later they had told me I *should* have remembered, at the age I was then, and that their saying this had suggested I did remember. But I do know, and they would not, that her breath was bad, that when she knelt down to do one up in front it was all one could do to stand there.

No one except he could have this immediate knowledge. It is part of the 'chain of feelings' linking him as he wrote with him then. It is the *same person* who was buttoned up by the maid, and who writes and who is now recreated as a single individual for us, as we read. It is his purely personal direct knowledge that alone could answer Goethe's question 'Was it memory?'

We cannot dispute the fact that there is such a thing as the personal knowledge which constitutes memory. The question remains, however, why it is that we value so highly the truth contained in such knowledge, and why this value attaches not only to what we may know about ourselves, but what others tell us that they know about *them*selves. Why do we want to discover such memory-truths, not only about ourselves but about others too?

People who write their autobiographies honestly, genuinely attempting to uncover this kind of immediate knowledge of their past, sometimes suggest, if called on to explain their motives, that what they write of themselves may somehow be *helpful* to other people. Such a claim is almost certainly mistaken. We do not, as a rule, learn lessons from other people's pasts; it is hard enough to learn from our own. But let us, all the same, consider one such claim.

Stephen Spender, in the introduction to his autobiography *World within World* (London, Faber and Faber, 1950: reissued 1985), wrote as follows:

> An autobiographer is really writing a story of two lives: his life as it appears to himself, from his own position, when he looks out at the world from behind his eye-sockets; and his life as it appears from outside, in the eyes of others; a view which tends to become in part his own view of himself also, since he is influenced by those others. An account of the interior view would be entirely subjective; and of the exterior would hardly be autobiography, but biography of oneself, on the hypothesis that someone can know about himself as if he were another person. However the great problem of autobiography remains, which is to create the true tension between these inner and outer, subjective and objective worlds.

The distinction between 'subjective' and 'objective', a dichotomy much loved by armchair philosophers, and notorious for shedding darkness rather than light, does not, I think, help here to explain what Spender means. He is, on the one hand, drawing a distinction between autobiography and history, between an 'interiorized' and an 'externalized' account of a life. On the other hand, he is attempting to explain the power that an autobiography may have to make the truth concerning an individual, known by memory only to himself, nevertheless true universally. He continues his explanation in a way that seems implausible. 'I have tried', he writes, 'to be as truthful as I can . . . and to write of experiences from which I feel I · have learned how to live . . . I believe obstinately that if I am able to write with truth about what has happened to me, this can help others who have to live through the same sort of thing.' Because of this essentially didactic theory of autobiography, that its value is to be useful, he does not hold that recollections of childhood are of any special interest.

> Many autobiographies have irritated me when I wanted to read about the writer's achievements, by beginning with a detailed account of his early days, forcing me to wade through a morass . . . of nurses, governesses, first memories, before I get to what really

interests me. Certainly masterpieces have been written about child-hood; but these are chiefly important for the light they throw on childhood in general, and they are not especially illuminating as the autobiography of particular individuals. That autobiographers have to begin by plunging into their earliest memories is surely an unnecessary convention.

It is perhaps worth noting, however, that Spender's account of his relations with his own grandmother, though not dating only from his earliest childhood, is the most moving and obviously true part of the book. But, of course, we do not learn from it how to live. Moreover, it is certainly true that we shall not learn how to conduct our lives by entering the childhood of an L. E. Jones or a Henry Green. But this is simply because to teach in this way is not the purpose of autobiography, however obstinately Spender may assert that it is. To say of something that it is a universal truth or that the understanding of it has a universal value does not mean that we learn from it what we ought to do, nor that we can relate it to circumstances likely to recur in our own lives. Spender's way of drawing the distinction between the particular and the general is mistaken. If something is known directly, recalled vividly, by an author, then *my* imagination can cause *me* to grasp that very truth, through *his* described memory of it. His imagination and mine show the universal in the particular.

This may be illustrated by what is probably the greatest master-piece about childhood ever written, Joyce's *Portrait of the Artist as a Young Man*. (That it is officially a novel makes it no less a work of memory, just as Proust's novel is.) There is a passage near the beginning where Stephen Daedalus at school, a little boy, has had his glasses broken on the Ash Path. He has written home to his father for another pair, and has meanwhile been excused from reading by Father Parnall. When Father Dolan, the Prefect of Studies, comes into the classroom, Stephen is beaten for idleness because he is not reading. Later, with great courage, he manages to go to the Rector to complain. The brilliance of all of this narrative, and of this part in particular, could not exist without the power of memory. For what we are given is an exact representation of how the scene appeared to an ignorant, pathetic, helpless child who knew nothing whatever of the world, but, as children do, had a strong sense of justice. 'It was easy, what he had to do', he reflected at lunch. 'All he had to do, when the dinner was over, and he came out in his turn, was to go on walking not out to the corridor but up the staircase on the right that led up to the castle.' Then the fellows stood up. They had all told him to go to the Rector, but, he thought, they would not go themselves. Then he was walking out in his turn. He had to decide. It was impossible to go. But why had Father Dolan had to ask his name twice? 'It was his own name he should have made fun of if he wanted to make fun."Dolan". It was like the name of a woman that washed clothes.' And so, reflecting in anger, he found himself walking along to the Rector's study. When it was all over and the Rector had promised that the mistake would be put right, he had his triumph with the older fellows. But he decided he would not triumph over Father Dolan. He went out, thinking how he would be kind to him, not proud. And thinking of this, he went out alone to the part of the grounds where he could smell the turnips and hear the sound of the cricket balls as the fellows were practising in the nets.

There is no reason why this truthful narrative should be so moving, except that its whole intention is to tell the truth. It is a story which could not be told by imagination itself, but only by imagination and memory together. It is because of this ultimate collaboration, even perhaps identity, of imagination with memory that what was the truth for one small boy is a truth which we can all claim as our own. And yet the story belongs to Daedalus and not to us. Great autobiographical writing, we may conclude, is both particular and general. This goes for any truth about a person, oneself or another. This is the answer to Spender. It is in the last degree unlikely that any autobiography will serve as a warning or an example to others, or 'help' them in the way Spender envisaged. But if the balance between the 'subjective' and the 'objective' or, as I should rather say, between the particular and the universal, is achieved, what will be presented is a unique individual, whose knowledge of himself we can share. In Collingwood's sense, his experience will become ours. What we get from him is the pleasure of grasping his completeness and continuity, and of understanding the truth in what he writes; we do not get a lesson in how to behave. We could not get this pleasure (part of the deep happiness in memory that Proust had to explore) unless we could accept the truth he tells as belonging to *others* than just to *himself*. There is no such thing as truth that is not in this degree intelligible. For us to grasp this intelligibility we need, as Sartre saw, to exercise imagination. Without imagination, autobiography, even if it were written, would certainly not be read.

There is another autobiographer who, in exploring her motivation, comes very much nearer than Spender to a satisfactory analysis. Storm Jameson's autobiography (one of the best ever written) is called *Journey from the North* (London, Collins, 1969). In the preface, she writes as follows:

124

The man or woman who has lived an uncommon life, or has played a part in some great undertaking . . . need not offer any further reason why he or she wants to record it. Some other reason (or excuse) is needed when the life brought out to be judged is nothing out of the way. My first and less egotistical excuse is that my memory, an exceptionally good one, contains three ages, the one that ended in August 1914, the one between November 1918 and August 1945, and the present, which may or may not have much of a future. The second and stronger reason, no more and no less egotistical than the impulse to write a novel, is the wish to discover before it is too late what sort of a person I have been, without allowing vanity or cleverness to soften the outline of the creature. I am an accomplished professional novelist and nothing . . . would have been easier for me than to draw a portrait which, without telling a single lie, would be dishonest from beginning to end, intelligent, charming, interesting, and a lie. I have tried to write with perfect sincerity, without malice towards others or myself . . . a degree of failure was implicit in the effort from the start, and a degree of distortion, however many precautions I took not to lie. But if I had not thought the effort worthwhile, to others besides myself, I should not have made it. It is improbable that the glass I have been looking into for the last four or five years reflects only my own mind and heart.

I have quoted this passage at length because it seems to me to contain so much of the truth. The analogy with novel-writing is hinted at (and again we are reminded of Sartre's 'true novel'); the desire to present a person who has existed continuously through time; the sense that this will be, not useful, but *satisfying* to the reader, as any recognition of truth is satisfying; the realization that for a 'pure' autobiography, as opposed to the memoir, to succeed, it is not an 'interesting' or 'eventful' life that is necessary, but the search after truth through memory; and finally the acknowledgement that an individual, imaginatively and truthfully explored, is more than just an individual. The general is found *in* the particular. The value we attach to memory expressed in language has hardly ever been more accurately identified.*

An autobiography may, of course, like a diary, fall into Bad Faith. Indeed, the autobiographer is more likely than the diarist to deceive

---

* Anthony Burgess (*Little Wilson and Big God*, London, Heinemann, 1987) of his reason for writing his autobiography: '. . . this is allegory in the original Greek sense of "speaking otherwise", presenting others in the shape of myself.'

himself. The risk is the price he has to pay for his relative detachment, the standing back to survey his life so far, which must precede his starting to write. It is, in any case, never easy to get things right, or tell it as it was, especially since, by choosing his language, the autobiographer is not only crystallizing, but to some extent creating, his past. He must choose, too, what tone he is going to adopt in talking about himself. Is he to be dispassionate, forgiving, or ironic? Irony, a protection against the possible charge of taking himself too seriously, or really believing in his own feelings and thoughts, is often a coward's way out. No one can ridicule a writer who may, after all, be ridiculing himself. But this, too, may be a kind of deception. There are difficulties, then, in autobiography. And yet it is in this genre that we may, above all, see the continuity that constitutes a human person. For the pleasures of memory are here brought to bear, to make up the story of a life. It is to the concept of *story* that we must turn now, in the final chapter.

7

The Story of a Life

If diaries are the raw materials of written lives, the essence of each day encapsulated as far as possible in truthful words, to prevent their escape, then autobiography is the story constructed out of this material. To create a story, both memory and imagination must be deployed, and autobiography is the place where, more than any other, their functions overlap. For a story is essentially a human creation. In an unpeopled universe, even if events occurred and changes took place, there would be no stories. Dan Jacobson, in his amazingly clear and apparently true volume of autobiographical essays (*Time and Time Again*, London, André Deutsch, 1985), expresses this point in his introduction:

> The pieces in this volume have been called 'autobiographies' for the simplest reason. In every one of them I have tried to be as faithful to my recollections as I possibly could be. At the same time, in writing the individual sections of the book, I wanted not only to tell the truth, as far as I knew it, about experiences I had been through or people with whom I had been involved, but also to produce *tales*, real stories, narratives which would provoke the readers' curiosity and satisfy it; which would appear to begin naturally, develop in a surprising and persuasive manner, and come to an end no sooner or later than they should.

He goes on later to say that the advantage of writing autobiography in an episodic style is that it would preserve in the form of stories 'something of the erratic or fitful nature of memory, and hence something of its intensity too'. Finally he refers to the continuity implicit in the writing of such 'tales'. 'In virtually every instance, my knowledge of what happened after such (single) episodes, or decades before them, became an essential and explicit part of the narrative itself. Only then would it seem to be truly autonomous, self-sufficient, able to carry within itself all it needed by way of context.' A story entails the continuous existence of the hero of it, through his lifetime. Only thus does it have any meaning.

It is not necessary for a story to be written down for it to exist as such. A story has to be told, but we may tell it to ourselves (though it must always be conceivable that we should tell it to others). But even if we tell our own story to ourselves, the story is a construct, a work of art; and that is why memory by itself, without imagination, is not enough. Every story needs a central figure and a plot. This plot will develop through time. When we are telling our own story the central figure is, of course, ourself, and the plot is our life, regarded from the point we have arrived at. My aim in this chapter is to concentrate again on memory itself, saying nothing further about written accounts in autobiographies or the *aides-mémoire* constituted by diaries (even though a good deal of the evidence about the nature of memory must be drawn from these sources). The peculiar value we attach to discursive memory, the recollection of what things were like, seems to derive from its connection with imagination in the developing story of a life. It is this connection that I wish to explore somewhat further in my final chapter.

The story of a life needs someone whose life it is, who 'has' or 'has had' the experiences and the emotions recalled. Why do we use the verb 'to have' in this context? Just as it is impossible to think of an experience without someone whose experience it is, who 'has' it, so a memory cannot be conceived without someone who 'has' it. Is my memory mine, therefore, as a kind of possession? My past may be thought to be stored away in my memory, as my marmalade is in my larder; and, in cliché terms, for the old, their memories may be 'all they have'. But the relation between me and my past is not like any other kind of ownership. In the case of other things that I own, I may always, if I want to, give them away, share them or sell them to someone else. But though in one sense I may share my memories, I cannot transfer them to another owner. Indeed, to say that they are mine does not necessarily suggest ownership at all. We understand what it means to call something 'mine' even though the exact relation between me and it may differ in different cases. We can understand in what sense someone may be 'my' doctor, someone else 'my' debtor, someone else 'my' child. We must try to see what special relationship is referred to when I speak of a memory, or a past, or a life, as 'mine'.

The question has been raised whether, if brain-transplants became possible, and part or all of my brain were transferred, as one of my kidneys might be, you would now have my memories belonging as they did with my brain (see chapter 4).

Everything we have said about personal identity makes it clear that my brain (any or all of it) is part of my body, that is, of me. All the experiences, including memories, that I have by means of my brain are 'my' experiences. If all or part of my brain were placed in your skull, it would now become yours, an aspect of you, and all experiences you had by means of it would be 'your' experiences. If among your future experiences, after the transplant, you had some alien 'memory-like' experiences, derived from the days when the brain you now have was mine; if, for instance, connections were made between the present and a past you never actually experienced, and you were 'reminded' of things that had never happened to you, still you would have to accommodate these as your somewhat mysterious memories. The past suggested or vaguely recalled would have to be thought of as your past. It would be like being reminded of something you experienced only in a dream. My dream-past is, after all, a kind of shadow-past, recalled, perhaps, in images of places I have never physically visited, or events I have never physically participated in. This, or something like it, is the way we should be forced to describe such cases, if they could ever occur, unless we were prepared to return to Cartesian dualism, and say that your mind and mine could be identical, though our bodies were still two. But such dualism has been rejected (see chapter 1).

So being the subject either of a present experience or of a memory-experience is a non-transferable condition. What I have you cannot have. On the other hand, insofar as having an experience or a memory is bound up with having a language in which to describe it (however difficult the attempts to describe it may be), what I have you can share. Indeed, P. F. Strawson (*Individuals*, London, Methuen, 1959, chapter 5) argues that we could not ascribe experiences to ourselves as subject unless we were prepared also to ascribe them to others, in principle, if not in fact. This is a logical or linguistic point. The term 'fear', for example, or 'recalled fear' means the same whether I use it of myself (ascribe the experience to myself) or of another. There are not two senses of the word 'fear', a first-person and a second- or third-person sense. Since words like 'fear' are intelligible, and are intended to communicate an unequivocal meaning, if I am said to be the subject of some such experience then others must also, potentially, be subject to it as well, even if as a matter of empirical history they have never experienced that particular emotion.

Among emotions are, of course, recalled emotions. If I can, in principle, ascribe to you all the experiences, emotions and recalled emotions that I can ascribe to myself, in what sense are my recalled emotions, or memories of emotion, 'mine'? What makes them mine rather than yours? The answer is that only their causal history makes them mine (see chapter 3).

There is an obvious ambiguity here which we must beware of. It is the notorious ambiguity of the idea of sameness. Memories, sensations, emotions and all experiences are subject to this ambiguity. There is a sense in which you could feel the same pain as I do, if you too had broken your arm, and your nervous system was structurally similar to my own. You could feel the same fear as I do when a face apears at the window, if you, like me, had grown up with a peculiar horror of such a thing. You and I could have the same memories if we had been at school together. It is out of such sameness of experience that all human sympathy and all human understanding derives. But in another sense, since my body is spatially distinct from yours, your pain and mine must be different. This is to say that your pain necessarily has a different causal history. The nervous system affected, though structurally similar to mine, is different, a different specimen of the same kind. And so the causal nature of a memory-experience is the reason why in one sense two people cannot have identically the same memories, but only memories whose starting point is the same. But we may share our memories by using intelligible words to locate their origin or starting point; to describe, that is, what they are memories *of*. If I can learn from your memories, it is because, both being human and in that sense 'speaking the same language', we may enter imaginatively into someone else's world. In one sense, by imagination, I may adopt your point of view. In another literal and physiological sense your point of view is yours, just as your eyes are yours and mine are mine.

So, being myself and not you or any other person, I lead my own life; and I may think of the life I have led as a story with a plot, albeit not yet complete. I may say to myself 'I have done all these things, and experienced all this, and come out here.' To think thus is a source of deep satisfaction, and we must try to explore the reason why this is so.

Richard Wollheim in an article entitled 'On Persons and their Lives' (in *Explaining Emotions*, ed. Amelie Rorty, University of California Press, 1980) attempts to answer this question by an appeal to psychoanalytic theory. His explanation is worth considering, since though it is, in my view, mistaken, nevertheless in its reliance on the causal nature of memory, it comes near the truth. Wollheim argues that we may regard humans as biological or as mental lives. The person who is 'most wholly integrated' is the person whose memories (part of his mental life) have 'due influence' over his present and his future, past, present and future being biologically connected, and also mentally experienced as connected. The story of a life can be told at whatever moment the teller chooses to look back over it, and to tell the story is to assert both mental and biological unity, or connectedness. Wollheim holds, rightly, that no account of a person could be complete unless it paid attention to how that person has developed through time. Thus my memories are essential to my account of myself, incorporated in the story of my life, of which, of course, I am the central figure.

Wollheim holds that psychoanalytic theory is uniquely efficient in providing such a historical perspective on the unique person. For he says it undertakes to show *how* the past affects, even determines, the present and the future of the individual. Moreover, besides its efficiency with regard to, as it were, the mechanics of the causation, psychoanalytic theory, in Wollheim's view, can also explain the satisfaction we feel when we recognize the causal influence of our past on our present. For those humans who are 'duly influenced' by their past, and recognize that this is so, are ideal, or 'fully integrated', humans. The value terms 'Duly', 'Integrated' and 'Ideal' arise out of psychoanalytic theory itself.

Now to explain values in terms of psychology is, as Wollheim agrees, 'naturalism'. Naturalistic value-theory is to be contrasted with those theories which would derive values from something quite separate from the ordinary world of nature (such as pure reason, or divine command); or with those theories which would argue that values need not have any common intelligible derivation at all, but are all passing whims or fashions, inexplicable and entirely relative to particular people, times or places. It is certainly not because of its naturalism that I would dispute Wollheim's conclusion. For if we are to give any intelligible account of why it is that we value something, in this case memory, as highly as we do, it must be assumed that all humans share certain common, deep and continuing sources of pleasure. It is a kind of explanation of the value we attach to something to say 'this is the sort of thing people enjoy'. And often we may feel that there is no more to be said. We have reached an ultimate source of pleasure. This is indeed 'naturalism'. Wollheim himself puts it thus:

> A naturalism that deserves consideration is any that can show how our values . . . derive from certain more primitive or elementary ways in which we regard those feelings, desires, dispositions that physical composition and our personal histories have given us . . . And it is a naturalism that not only deserves consideration but can command our adherence, which can further show that these more

primary attitudes and the acceptances and rejections that they give rise to are crucial to our development; so that unless we concurred with them we should be immobilized.

A 'concurrence' or acceptance of the influence of our past upon us is just such a crucial case, he argues. 'It is nothing less than the acceptance of ourselves as the persons we are.'

Wollheim is not, obviously, saying that we need psychoanalytic theory to show us that we rely on our memories, or to enable us to accept the teaching of memory. All animals so rely; and we know we should be lost without such reliance, in all practical aspects of our lives. In this sense we have the most excellent reason to value memory, and to grant its due influence. If I can't remember where I left my glasses, and I need them now, I am indeed 'immobilized', in Wollheim's phrase. If I can remember where I left them, then I shall certainly go and look for them there. If I don't, it would be almost impossible to believe that I really remembered, since my failure to seek them in that place would be totally irrational. In this way not only does the past influence what I do, but my consciousness of the past is crucial in guiding my present actions. I acknowledge this influence and am thankful for it.

Psychoanalytic theory is invoked, however, on the grounds that it alone can show us the 'persons that we are', by uncovering a different aspect of our memories. It can not only uncover memories which, in practice, we might have suppressed or failed to acknowledge without the aid of analysis, but, more important, the theory of analysis will, it is claimed, reveal the significance to us of these and other memories. The theory is supposed to show the *emotional content* of certain memories, and hence their meaning. It allows us beneficially to 'concur' with the influence of the past on us, by understanding these meanings. The value of such understanding is that we become more fully 'integrated' people, and are not liable to be 'immobilized'.

The value we attached to accepting the influence upon us of our memories, to the understanding of their meaning, is thus essentially practical. It enables us to live better than we would otherwise live. Psychoanalytic theory is not mere theory; it is intended to have a therapeutic outcome for all those who adopt it. We derive values from it because we accept this outcome. It is as if we said that we derive the value of health (which everyone would agree was good) from the fact that everyone prefers to be healthy rather than unhealthy. So it is supposed to be common ground that it is preferable for each individual to be 'integrated' rather than the reverse. The penalty for non-integration is 'immobility'.

This 'immobility' is, obviously, metaphorical; but even granted that, it is not at all clear what it means. In any case there is a further and fatal drawback to Wollheim's theory. The value of acknowledging our causal dependence on memory is, in his view, a wholly individual value. I shall live my life better if I acknowledge the meanings *for me* of my own memories. I may recommend that you too adopt psychoanalytic theory, so that you too may benefit; but the good that will supposedly come to each of us will be practical for each of us. To uncover the significance of my memories is of use to me and me alone (just as it is directly in my interest, and only mine, to remember where I've left my glasses). Such self-orientated benefit fails, I think, adequately to explain the nature of the pleasure we experience in recognizing and exploring our own memories.

Richard Coe, in his study of the autobiographies of childhood (op. cit., p. 109), makes the same point:

> Freudian psychology . . . is irremediably one-dimensional, positivistic . . . and utilitarian; it takes no account of that 'second reality', as Gide terms it, which is the essence of childhood revisited, nor is it in any way concerned with intuitive meanings and ultimate significances. For the poet . . . this meaningfulness demands to be situated in a context outside himself; otherwise it is futile. It must be felt to relate, if not to a transcendental dimension in the usual sense, then at least to other human beings and other experiences: to a communal subconscious perhaps, to an inheritance from past generations, to an all-embracing mythology . . . more real than any 'real' experience, and more mysterious in its workings than any run-of-the-mill psychological determinism.

The point that Coe makes could perhaps be made by introducing again the idea of *imagination*. Telling our story, to ourselves or others, is, as we have seen, the outcome of a collaboration between memory and imagination; indeed, in this context, the two are not wholly to be separated. For the creative construction of a story involves seeking out what is significant, what is to feature as part of the plot. When we relive something in recollection, experiencing again what it was like, we are discovering a truth; and truth, even if it is a truth concerning ourselves, is necessarily in one sense general. If genuinely true, it has meaning universally. Now the primary function of imagination is to perceive in the particular what is universal, to see more in the individual event or object than would meet the superficial or unimaginative eye. The objects of imagination are often, though not always, objects that are absent, in time or place, and imagination is concerned to discover the significance of such objects. As Coe suggests, objects that are absent in time, if they are to be worth contemplating, must seem to have a universal significance, that is, they must be the objects of imagination as well as of memory. And if we consider them so, they will yield not just a means by which I may improve my own life, but *understanding*, a quite general insight into how things are, not only from my standpoint, but absolutely universally.

To say this is not to deny what has already been asserted, that the first requirement of memory is that it should be *my own*. Indeed, the discovery of the individual 'me', to be the subject of all future events and memories of events, is often reported as itself a memory of central significance. Without the recognition of this 'I' to be the subject of all future experiences, there can be nothing on to which to latch the kind of memory which is self-conscious recognition. As I value myself, so I value my life, the past that I have.

There is a good example of the sudden recognition of this subject, 'I', in the first volume of Anthony Powell's autobiography (*Infants of the Spring*, London, Heinemann, 1976). He records an occasion in London when he was five or six and had just come back to the flat where he lived from a walk in the park.

> After the park and the street the interior of the building seemed very silent. A long beam of sunlight, in which small particles of dust swam about, all at once slanted through an upper window on the staircase, and struck the opaque glass panels of the door. On several occasions recently I had been conscious of approaching the brink of some discovery; an awareness that nearly became manifest and then withdrew. Now the truth came flooding in with the dust-infested sunlight. There was no doubt about it. I was me.

> > So rounds he to a separate mind
> > From whence clear memory may begin,
> > And through the frame that binds him in
> > His isolation grows defined.

Anthony Powell's great discovery was tied to a present moment, caused perhaps by an especially acute present vision. But it was seen to have consequences for the future, for the whole story of his life. I remember a similar revelation in my own case when at about the same age, five or six, having misbehaved, I was shut in the night-nursery as a punishment. Not unmixed with defiance, perhaps, I had the same sudden recognition that I was me, and always would be, and that it would be impossible for anyone ever to take that identity away from me whatever else they might take. The revelation was accompanied by a sense of extreme, blissful happiness. There is a similar fictional description of such a recognition in Richard Hughes's novel *A High Wind in Jamaica*. (London, New Phoenix Library, 1956, first published 1929)

In a child, such feelings of uniqueness may well be connected more with the future than the past. But they may be equally closely linked to the past, and the older someone is the more his sense of identity is indistinguishable from his sense of his own past. His past is what he is, rather than what he 'has'. His memories have been caused by physical happenings within his body (including, of course, his brain); and his body is still *his* body. There is a causal link, joining him then with him now. This is the firm factual basis of our sense of continuity with the past. On the other hand, since cause precedes its effect and is distinct from it, the past, causally linked to the individual through memory and other bodily changes, is necessarily separate from the present; the person who remembers is detached from it.

Sartre, in *Being and Nothingness* ('Temporality', pp. 107ff.), discusses this ambiguity, the sense in which a person *is* the person he *was*, and the sense in which he *is not* that person. If humans were without consciousness, then their history would 'belong' to them in a quite different sense. It would simply have brought it about that they were now in the physical state they are in, just as the mode of manufacture of a nail brings it about that now, when someone wishes to hammer it into the wall, it bends. The learning processes of animals are often viewed in this light, if those animals are not human. Their genetic inheritance combined with the experiences they have been subjected to together determine what they do. As I suggested in chapter 1, it is not certain that this type of behaviourism is an adequate account of the relation between an animal's past and its present, at least in the case of intelligent animals like rats; in any case, the difference between a rat or an octopus and a nail is that we are prepared to speak of the animals learning from experience. They are conscious of their experiences in a way that nails are not.

Whatever may be true of other animals, in the case of humans at any rate, although the causal nature of memory and of learning entails that their history belongs to them in the way that the history of the nail belongs to it, this does not exhaust the way in which it belongs. Humans think of their past as theirs not only because it has caused them to be where they are, but also because of the *conjunction* of factors which make them able to identify their past as their own. The human being, in Sartre's terminology, is both 'in-itself' (a physical existent, a body as much as a nail is) and also 'for-itself', a consciousness. It is this dual existence that explains the ambiguity of the past. Only beings-for-themselves 'have' their pasts. Insofar as my past is still relevant to my present (as, for instance, when I still bear a grudge against someone who *has* injured me) then my past is me. But, in another sense, in Sartre's less than elegant words, 'the past is the ever-growing totality of the in-itself which we are'. When I die, I no longer have a past. I am, if thought of at all, thought of as a complete thing, like a nail or a tree, caused to be as I was by the things that happened to me. Until we are dead 'we are not identical with the in-itself. We are responsible for it. We have to be it.' In this sense as long as I am alive and conscious, I am my past, which is mine because it is viewed from the standpoint of my present. I am as much responsible for the way I see my past, and the use I make of it, as I am for any aspect of my present situation. But there is also the truth that I cannot re-enact or change the past. This is the ambiguity which, according to Sartre, we constantly aware of.

We have reached here one of the salient facts about human beings which made it seem inevitable, long before Descartes, to signify in language itself some kind of dualism, some distinction between body and mind. Dualism is a way of noticing that body is, though a living thing, nevertheless something brought to the state it now is in by how it came into being, and what has happened to it; whereas a mind, from whatever particular standpoint in time, seems able to detach itself from the past, re-create it and use its re-creation for the planning of the future. It is the sense of freedom, and of the ability to look both backwards and forwards, that is the inspiration of dualism. It is also at the heart of the value we ascribe to the discovery that 'I am me'.

R. G. Collingwood developed a sense of history that gave an exalted role to the individual mind. In *Speculum Mentis* (*Speculum Mentis or the Map of Knowledge*, Oxford, Oxford University Press, 1924) he wrote (p. 301): 'A mind which knows its own change is by that very knowledge lifted above change. History, and the same is true of memory . . . is the mind's triumph over time. In the . . . process of thought, the past lives in the present, not as a mere "trace" or effect of itself on the physical organism, but as the object of the mind's historical knowledge of itself in an eternal present.' We may justifiably, each of us, think of the memory of our life as 'a triumph over time' in a way that the life itself was not. We turn our life into a story by remembering it, and any story, or history, is thus timeless; we can tell the story to ourselves again and again, and the truth it contains does not change.

There is no doubt that the pleasure, or joy, we feel in recollection is connected with such experienced 'timelessness', a timelessness which gives depth and point to our present life, as we remember. Virginia Woolf ('A Sketch of the Past', op. cit.) describes the effect of remembering thus:

> The past only comes back when the present runs so smoothly that it is like the sliding surface of a deep river. Then one sees through the surface to the depths. In those moments I find one of my greatest satisfactions, not that I am thinking of the past; but that it is then that I am living most fully in the present. For the present when backed by the past is a thousand times deeper than the present when it presses so close that you can feel nothing else, when the film on the camera reaches only the eye.

But it may still be asked whether the character of the experience we remember also contributes to the pleasure we feel, if we do, in recalling it. For instance, do we enjoy recalling childhood because of its own special character, the then brightness, freshness and novelty of our experience, or is this lustre something we add in recollection? There is no doubt that the 'clouds of glory' that the child brings to his experience are not mere inventions, added in the process of recollection. The case is more complicated than that. We can probably all remember the actual sharpness of sensation associated with childhood, our closeness to the ground, for example, giving us more pungent smells, more accurate and clear observation of small objects than most of us have had since, and the narrowness of our horizons, metaphorical as well as literal, giving intense significance to everyday objects, to quite ordinary tastes, textures and colours. Our emotions were more deeply engaged in what we experienced than they are likely to be later. A description of this intensity of sensations comes in Gwen Raverat's book *Period Piece* (London, Faber and Faber, 1952). Writing of Down House, where her Darwin relatives lived, she says:

> Everything there was different. And better.
>
> For instance, the path in front of the veranda was made of large round water-worn pebbles from some sea beach. They were not loose, but stuck down tight in moss and sand and were black and shiny as if they had been polished. I adored those pebbles. I mean literally, *adored*; worshipped. This passion made me feel quite sick sometimes. And it was adoration that I felt for the foxgloves at Down, and for the stiff red clay out of the Sandwalk clay-pit; and for the beautiful white paint on the nursery floor. This kind of feeling hits you in the stomach, and in the ends of your fingers, and it is probably the most important thing in life.

She is here describing, with great precision, what it was like at the time. But she goes on:

> Long after I have forgotten all my human loves I shall still remember the smell of a gooseberry leaf, or the feel of the wet grass on my bare feet; or the pebbles in the path. In the long run it is this feeling that makes life worth living, this which is the driving force behind the artist's need to create.

The joy in such remembering, then, is partly to be explained by the fact that things *were* as she described, and *were* 'adored', at the time. But the artist's need to create is satisfied by the *telling* of how it was, by the inclusion of these remembered loves in her story, by the re-creation of the ecstasy.

The pleasures that really existed in the past and the pleasures now of recalling them then are inextricably mixed. We cannot wholly separate the quality of the recollection (whether or not it presents itself in the form of an image) from the quality of what it is a recollection of. In Simone de Beauvoir's book *Old Age* (translated by Patrick O'Brien, London, Penguin, 1972) she quotes from Ionesco's *Journal en Miettes*:

> I remember the quarter of an hour's break at my primary school. A quarter of an hour! It was long and it was full, there was time to think of a game, play it right through and begin another . . . But next year was merely a word; and even if I did think that this next year might come, it seemed to me so far-off that it was not worth troubling about; it was as long as all eternity before next year would come round, which was much the same as not coming round at all.

Simone de Beauvoir comments:

> The reason why the emotional memories that restore childhood are so treasured is that for a fleeting instant they give us back a boundless future. A cock crows in the distance; I am walking in a meadow covered with hoar frost; all at once it is Meyrignac and there is a catch at my heart – this day now just beginning stretches out, a vast expanse, as far as the distant twilight; tomorrow is no more than an empty word. Eternity is my portion. And then suddenly it is not. I am back in my days when the years go by so fast.

Perceived time really is different for children; and in old age we can cheat ourselves momentarily by recalling what it felt like to be presented with such an endless present and infinite future. But a cheat is what it is. Again, Simone de Beauvoir (op. cit., p. 407) quotes Emmanuel Berl who wrote in *Sylvia*: 'My past escapes me. I tug at one end, I tug at the other, and all that stays in my hand is a rotten scrap of fraying cloth. Everything turns into a ghost or a lie. I can scarcely make myself out at all in the pictures my memory offers.' She adds:

> The past is not a peaceful landscape lying there behind me, a country in which I can stroll whenever I please, and which will gradually show me all its secret hills and dales. As I was moving forward, so it was crumbling. Most of the wreckage that can still be seen is colourless, distorted, frozen: its meaning escapes me. The past moves us for the very reason that it is past; but this too is why it so often disappoints us – we lived it in the present, a present rich in the future towards which it was hurrying; and all that is left is a skeleton.

If she makes a pilgrimage to visit some place where she had lived before, it is a disappointment. 'I shall never find my plans again, my hopes and fears. I shall not find myself.'

Such a melancholy account may seem a digression in an exploration of the pleasures of memory, and the high value we attach to our creations and re-creations of our own pasts. Simone de Beauvoir's lament can add nothing, it may be thought, to an attempt to account for the peculiar satisfaction of recollection. But we have to acknowledge that there is a sense in which what she says is both true and important. When I recall my past, although I may remember that there was, at the time, a decision to be made, action to be taken, hope of as yet undisclosed excitement in the then future, and though I may recall what it felt like to be presented with such choices and such hopes, what I cannot do is re-create the actual necessity for action or decision. If I recollect that forty or so years ago I had to decide what special subjects to take in my examinations, and even if I relive the agonies of indecision, or the excitements of embarking on something new, what I cannot do is make it necessary to *choose again*. In the past I was free; now, looking back on the past, my choices are determined. I can tell the story as it was; but I cannot change the plot at will.

Schopenhauer (*The World as Will and Representation*, translated by Ed. F. Payne, New York, Columbia University Press, 1985), one of the few philosophers to have been concerned with the value we attach to memory, held that the very feature of memory which made it, for Simone de Beauvoir, such a disappointment, was, on the contrary, that which gave it its charm for us. According to his epistemology, the knowledge we have of the everyday world, whether 'common sense' or science, is all 'interested' knowledge. We seek to know in order to explain and to change. We take for granted that some explanation is to be found (he calls this assumption 'the principle of sufficient reason'); and so we take for granted that we can, when we have explained it, manipulate the world according to our will and desire. The will, he holds, is a passion; a passion for the next thing. A man in the ordinary world, seeking knowledge, whether of science or common sense, is never satisfied. His search is restless because no sooner does he have it than he must act on it; and then immediately a new imperative arises, to take the next step, make the next change in his world. There is no peace, under the tyranny of will. 'But', Schopenhauer writes (op. cit., p. 192), 'when knowledge is snatched from the thraldom of the will, the attention is now no longer directed to the motives of willing, but comprehends things free from their relation to the will . . . then all at once peace comes to us of our own accord, and all is well with us. We celebrate the Sabbath of the penal servitude of willing; and the wheel of Ixion stands still.'

So it is possible to attain a different kind of knowledge, at least temporarily, knowledge not of how things work, why they exist or how to use them, but of what they are in themselves. It is difficult, of course, to imagine what such essential knowledge would be like. But the same is true of the timeless, spontaneous knowledge described by Bergson, the knowledge of essences conceived by Husserl, or indeed the knowledge of forms attained by the philosophers in Plato's Republic. To set up an ideal of knowledge, different from what passes under that name in ordinary life, is by no means a philosophical novelty.

Schopenhauer tells us that this kind of ideal knowledge is, first and foremost, aesthetic in character. It is in the knowledge of beauty in the arts or in nature that we attain the peaceful contemplation of things as they really are, and achieve the satisfaction we seek in vain in the ordinary practical business of life. Aesthetic knowledge is, he says, detached from all particular times and places. Where there is a pre-dominance of knowing over willing 'it is all one whether we see the setting sun from a prison or from a palace' (op. cit., p. 198). He adds:

> It is also that blessedness of will-less perception which spreads so wonderful a charm over the past and the distant, and by self-deception presents them in so flattering a light. For by our conjuring up in our minds days long past spent in a distant place, it is only the objects reached by our imagination, not the subject of will that carried around its incurable sorrows with it just as much then as it does now. But these are forgotten because, since, they have frequently made way for others . . . hence it happens that, especially

when we are more than usually disturbed by some want, the sudden recollection of past and distant scenes flits across our minds like a lost paradise.

The aesthetic attitude, adopted towards works of art or objects of natural beauty, is one of stillness. We require nothing from them. Nor do we require anything from our recollections. If we contemplate what we recollect, we shall see the reality of the things and places that we remember. *Now*, they are not mere tools for us to use, or launching-pads for some new enterprise, even though that is what they were when we originally experienced them.

Our separation from our past, then, our ability to stand back from it without its making demands on us, is precisely what gives us peace and satisfaction in contemplating it. A universal truth may thus be revealed, not a truth relative to our purposes, which have become irrelevant. The very feature that disappoints Simone de Beauvoir is the essential and satisfying centre of recollection for Schopenhauer. But, in one respect, he is in agreement with her. Simone de Beauvoir complained that, in recollection, she would never find herself. Schopenhauer holds that this is no matter for complaint. Indeed the aesthetic attitude that we may adopt to our own past in recollection is *necessarily* impersonal, and this is its merit. For the world of representation, whether in art or in the images of memory, is completely separate from the world of will. The representation is 'pure object'. It has no element of the *subject who represents* in it. The world of will, on the other hand, is completely subjective and relative. It is centred on what *I* want and what *I* need to have. We can attain objective knowledge only if we put ourselves completely out of the picture. In memory, Schopenhauer says, 'the imagination recalls merely what was objective, not what was individually subjective, and we imagine that something objective stood before us then just as pure and undisturbed by any relation to the will as its image now stands in the imagination'. The identity of recollecting with the contemplation of the aesthetic is complete. 'We can withdraw from all suffering just as well through present as through distant objects, whenever we raise ourselves to a purely objective contemplation of them and are able to produce the illusion that only those objects are present, not we ourselves. The world as representation alone remains; the world as will has disappeared.'

But Schopenhauer (and for that matter Simone de Beauvoir) is certainly mistaken. For recollection cannot consist in the pure contemplation of events or actions without an author, even if these events and actions take place in some past. The past must be *somebody's* past if it is to be recalled. My memory must include the consciousness of myself engaging in the activities, 'having' the feelings or sensations that I remember. It is a contradiction to suppose that I could put myself out of the picture, and still be remembering. Indeed, as we have seen, it is because what I remember is mine, is part of *my* life, and no one else's, that it carries with it the peculiar satisfaction whose source we are trying to trace. It is only if I find myself in my memories that they are memories in the full sense, and that they can bring their distinctive joy.

Is the paradise thus glimpsed illusory? Even if, as children, we did perceive things with a now-lost sharpness and vivacity, even if there was something uniquely exciting about the slow passage of time, and the apparently unending future, we did not actually inhabit paradise in those days. We had our ups and downs and, often, long stretches of boredom. It is time to attempt some conclusions on the nature of this paradise.

As we saw (see chapter 5), Wordsworth believed that the joy of memory came through the contemplation of the world as image. Images of the absent, called up, perhaps, by things present, and half-mixed with present sights and sounds, were, according to his theory, the only source of understanding, the well from which to draw the water of life itself. Memory and creative imagination could not be distinguished. They worked together to enable us to understand and interpret the forms or images of experience. But simply because the separation of past from present remains, there is in memory, necessarily, a sense of loss: we look back to a country to which we cannot return.

> Turn wheresoe'er I may,
> By night or day,
> The things which I have seen I now can see no more

In an unpublished thesis, John Waterfield expresses it thus:

> Imagination can recall the past, trace the relations between the then and the now, so indicating the unity of imaginative form that transcends the difference . . . The Fall is the myth of separation from paradise . . . Against the Fall, Wordsworth's chief resource is memory.

Memory then comes as a saviour. Like a Messiah, it is to save us from the otherwise inevitable destruction brought by death and time. Just as for Proust it was not the original experience but the reliving of the experience which gave rise to so intense a joy, so for Wordsworth too it is essential to the poet's triumph over time that the past, though still past, should be lived again.

The concept of the re-creation of life is central to this view of memory and imagination, and explains the value that we attach to recollection. What is re-created is my life. But this has significance, as both Wordsworth and Proust understood, not just for me. The active and creative, and also the universal aspect of memory is suggested in another way by Virginia Woolf. In 'A Sketch of the Past' (op. cit., p. 71) she recounts three exceptional memories which stood out from the 'cotton wool' or 'non-being' of her childhood. Each memory was of an emotional experience that came as a violent shock. 'Something', she wrote, 'happened so violently that I have remembered it all my life.' One of these shocks was an occasion in the garden at St Ives in her early childhood.

> I was looking at the flower bed by the front door; 'That is the whole', I said. I was looking at a plant with a spread of leaves; and it seemed suddenly plain that the flower itself was a part of the earth; that a ring enclosed what was the flower; and that was the real flower; part earth; part flower. It was a thought I put away as being likely to be very useful to me later.

Of the three exceptional moments, she says: 'I often tell them over, or rather they come to the surface unexpectedly.' And she goes on to analyse their impact. 'When I said about the flower "That is the whole", I felt that I had made a discovery. I felt that I had put away in my mind something that I should go back [to], to turn over and explore.' And she says:

> a shock is at once . . . followed by the desire to explain it. I feel that I have had a blow; but it is not . . . simply a blow from an enemy hidden behind the cotton wool of daily life; it is or will become the revelation of some order; it is a token of some real thing behind appearances; and I make it real by putting it into words. It is only by putting it into words that I make it whole; . . . it gives me . . . great delight to put the severed parts together. Perhaps this is the strongest pleasure known to me.

The writer's role, then, is to re-create the vision, the intuition of truth, that belongs to these remembered 'shocks'. From less dramatic, less episodic, recollections, too, it is possible, Virginia Woolf holds, to reconstruct a life, her own life, but with innumerable links to other lives, not directly part of her own experience. Her recollections of fishing will serve as an example (op. cit., p. 134). 'Sometimes lines would be handed us; baited by gobbets cut from fish; and the line thrilled in one's fingers as the boat tossed and shot through the water; and then – how can I convey the excitement? – there was a little leaping tug; then another; up one hauled; up through the water at length came the white twisting fish.' The passion for the thrill and the tug was, she says, the most acute passion she then knew. But her father made it clear that he did not like to see fish caught; and so, without apparent resentment, she learned not to want to catch them any more.

> And from the memory of my own passion I am still able to construct the sporting passion. It is one of those invaluable seeds – for as it is impossible to have every experience, one must make do with seeds – germs of what might have been. I pigeon-hole 'fishing' thus with other momentary glimpses, like those glances I cast into basements when I walk in London streets.

If it were not for the visions afforded by memories of one's own life, one would not be able to understand the lives of others. The glimpses into the basements would have no significance unless they overlapped and reflected the significance of personal memories.

A life, or lives, lived in episodes and through time, is, Virginia Woolf has no doubt, the subject matter of the creative and re-creative imagination. She writes:

> Always a scene has arranged itself: representative; enduring. This confirms me in my instinctive notion: (it will not bear arguing about; it is irrational) the sensation that we are sealed vessels afloat on what it is convenient to call reality; and at some moments, the sealing matter cracks; in floods reality; that is, these scenes – for why do they survive undamaged year after year unless they are made of something comparatively permanent? (op. cit., p. 142)

Virginia Woolf was, of course, recalling her past, as a writer; and, like Wordsworth in *The Prelude*, or Proust in his novel, exploring not only the 'joy' of the creativity of memory, but the way this joy had to be expressed in art. The same re-creation by the imagination/ memory, and the satisfaction that it brings has been explored by other people, however, who are not writers, or artists of any kind. For all of them, the fascination of the past is its relevance to and connections with the present. These people have not finished with their past; it still lives in them. Anthony Palmer, writing about 'The Point of Autobiography' (*Proceedings of the Aristotelian Society*, supplementary volume, 1979), puts it thus: 'The man who says to himself "Now that it is all behind me, let me see if I can get it straight for myself" is deluding himself in thinking that it is all behind him. The self for which he is trying to get it straight is his present self.' The continuity of 'selves' is crucial to the value of memory (and this is further proof of the wrongness of Schopenhauer's analysis of this value).

The sense of continuity in memory may be amply illustrated by the conversations with the aged, recorded in Ronald Blythe's book *The View in Winter* (London, Allen Lane, 1979). The people to whom he talked return many times to the landscape of their childhood, and their childhood has become a story that they tell; but it is essentially, not merely accidentally, their own story, the story of their lives. They have had, and have still got, their lives. For example, an eighty-two-year-old former farrier says, 'I balance things up when I can. I've got no work and no wife, but I've got what I've done, haven't I? We've all got that, haven't we?' There was a retired gamekeeper who said 'I remember it all most particularly; Aunt, Jacko my monkey, her Grace, the round houses which the Duke built and all the fun we had. It was a long way back in my lifetime but I lived it.' Many of the conversations Ronald Blythe recorded confirm that the sense of personal identity, of continuity through time, is so strong that it carries with it the conviction that, in some way, the people telling their lives are not old, not in the way that other people, seen from the outside, are old. They are not completely described by the adjective 'old', and are often horrified to be treated as if they were. They are certain that, despite all appearances, they are the same as they were. An eighty-four-year-old retired schoolmaster says 'Old age doesn't necessarily mean that one is entirely old'; and 'I tend to look upon other old men as *old men* – and not include myself.' And a retired teacher of ninety-one says 'Of course I can't walk very far but the inside person who can't walk very far is still the same young woman who rambled for miles and miles.' Such conversations, and such thoughts, are familiar enough.

Acute awareness of identity, of our own personal identity over time, is not incompatible with the universality of truth which Schopenhauer ascribes to the knowledge derived from recollection. Nor is he mistaken in relating this universality to aesthetic knowledge, or aesthetic understanding. When we intensely enjoy an aesthetic experience, we have a sense of completeness, a feeling that nothing could be changed. Everything that we have experienced by eye or ear is fitting. It hangs together to be an individual and a perfection. There is an analogy here with the pleasure we may have in constructing the story of our life: the parts fit together. One element in the plot suggests, gives meaning to, the others. It *was* so and could not have been otherwise, given the individual life that it is. It is as if there was a pattern, unpredictable before the plot unfolded, but now seen to be intelligible. A particular 'scene', to use Virginia Woolf's word, makes sense only if you know who they were who participated in the scene; and, in recollecting, you do know. You know that, from your point of view, the central figure was yourself. You 'had' the experience.

Recollection, then, though connected, as one end of a continuum with another, to the kind of memory of which we are hardly aware as we go about our daily life ('Where did I leave my glasses?' 'How do you dial an international call?' 'Can I ride a bicycle?'), is an active and creative undertaking. It is the reconstruction of the story of a life in which episodes are fitted into a whole. If it gives us pleasure, the centre of that pleasure is the sense of continuity between then and now which makes the story one, and mine. It is, of course, easy, at times, to deny such continuity. One may say, like Simone de Beauvoir, 'I do not see myself in that person.' Like Proust, one may feel no identity when in love with the person not in love. The self *then* may seem so unlike the self *now* that it may seem tempting to say they are two different people. In such a mood, a mood of rejection of his past, a man may say that he now has nothing to do with that other person, the person who figures in that 'scene'. But, if he says this, he deceives himself. If he can reconstruct the scene in recollection, not simply knowing that it occurred, but in the crucial way knowing what it was like, then he must also know that he was that person, and that there is a causal continuity between him (his body) then, and him (his body) now. To understand his continuity, to grasp his own duration is to defeat time, for he has not finished with his past. It, with his present, together make the pattern. The plot embraces them both. Perhaps one of the consolations of old age is that, through memory, it makes artists of us all.

In conclusion, then, we may see that the consolations, or insights, of this art, the art of recollection, derive from two sources. First, whatever 'aesthetic' pleasures we get, whether from creating our own representations of things, or from understanding the representations of others, these pleasures, carry with them the realization that they are universal. Kant, in the *Critique of Judgment* (translated by J. C. Meredith, Oxford, Oxford University Press, 1911, p. 218), argued that in aesthetic judgement, though we speak of our own feelings, we nevertheless demand that these feelings, this subjectivity, should be shared. And so it is the certainty that we have come upon a universal truth that pleases us when we construct a story. If we also know that the story is true, that this is how things actually were, then that knowledge is far from value-free. It is a kind of knowledge that we seek, and prize above all when we have found it.

Secondly, when, in knowing the truth of the story, we also know that the central character in the plot was ourselves, we are possessed of the notion of continuity through time. We know that the particular physical object, ourself, has necessarily continued, otherwise our reconstruction of the plot would be historical or fictional; imagined, but not also remembered. The value we attach to recollection, then, derives from our physiological continuity with the past. It is the causal link between what happened *then* and what is happening in memory *now* which makes our memory a possession in which, as Proust said, we triumph over time.

Index